W9-AWO-528

"Careful," Grace called behind her just as Ryder slipped.

She had one second to wish he'd worn his combat boots instead of the cowboy boots that hadn't been made for this terrain. He tried to catch himself, but the rocks gave way and he barreled toward her.

"Out of the way!" He threw his weight to the side to avoid her, but she stood her ground and leaned into his path to catch him.

"Grace!"

He tumbled with her, then caught her somehow, his arms tight around her and holding her in place just as they would have gone over the edge of the precipice.

They were on the last large rock, she on the bottom and he on top of her. A long, hard drop below.

As he looked at her, his eyes were a soft, tawny brown, a contrast to his hard-muscled body. "Are you hurt?"

Dazed. A long time had passed since she'd last felt the weight of a man on top of her. And Ryder McKay was definitely no ordinary man.

DANA MARTON

THE SPY WORE SPURS

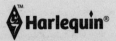
Harlequin®

TORONTO NEW YORK LONDON
AMSTERDAM PARIS SYDNEY HAMBURG
STOCKHOLM ATHENS TOKYO MILAN MADRID
PRAGUE WARSAW BUDAPEST AUCKLAND

If you purchased this book without a cover you should be aware
that this book is stolen property. It was reported as "unsold and
destroyed" to the publisher, and neither the author nor the
publisher has received any payment for this "stripped book."

A big thank-you goes to Pat Neff, who kindly shared her vast knowledge of South Texas,
and my fabulous editor, Allison Lyons.

My most sincere gratitude to Gayle Cochrane for giving Twinky her name,
and to Margaret Sholders who told me about her donut-eating cat. Many thanks to
Lana Manley Parks for giving Cookie a name, and to Maureen for naming Maureen J.
And my warmest appreciation to Lisa Boggs, Amanda Scott and Cheryl Bartholomew who
lent their names to Ryder's sisters. This book is dedicated to my readers, who are the best
people on earth, especially Deb Posey Chudzinski, Sarah Conerty Jordan,
Lena Gerber and all the ladies already mentioned above!

Recycling programs
for this product may
not exist in your area.

ISBN-13: 978-0-373-69631-4

THE SPY WORE SPURS

Copyright © 2012 by Dana Marton

All rights reserved. Except for use in any review, the reproduction or
utilization of this work in whole or in part in any form by any electronic,
mechanical or other means, now known or hereafter invented, including
xerography, photocopying and recording, or in any information storage
or retrieval system, is forbidden without the written permission of the
publisher, Harlequin Enterprises Limited, 225 Duncan Mill Road,
Don Mills, Ontario M3B 3K9, Canada.

This is a work of fiction. Names, characters, places and incidents are
either the product of the author's imagination or are used fictitiously,
and any resemblance to actual persons, living or dead, business
establishments, events or locales is entirely coincidental.

This edition published by arrangement with Harlequin Books S.A.

For questions and comments about the quality of this book
please contact us at Customer_eCare@Harlequin.ca.

® and TM are trademarks of the publisher. Trademarks indicated with
® are registered in the United States Patent and Trademark Office, the
Canadian Trade Marks Office and in other countries.

www.Harlequin.com

Printed in U.S.A.

ABOUT THE AUTHOR

Dana Marton is the author of more than a dozen fast-paced, action-adventure, romantic-suspense novels and a winner of a Daphne du Maurier Award of Excellence. She loves writing books of international intrigue, filled with dangerous plots that try her tough-as-nails heroes and the special women they fall in love with. Her books have been published in seven languages in eleven countries around the world. When not writing or reading, she loves to browse antiques shops and enjoys working in her sizable flower garden, where she searches for "bad" bugs with the skills of a superspy and vanquishes them with the agility of a commando soldier. Every day in her garden is a thriller. To find more information on her books, please visit www.danamarton.com. She loves to hear from her readers and can be reached via email at DanaMarton@DanaMarton.com.

Books by Dana Marton

HARLEQUIN INTRIGUE

*Mission: Redemption
**Defending the Crown

CAST OF CHARACTERS

Grace Cordero—She returns to the family ranch to spread her brother's ashes. But her time back home doesn't turn out as she expects. A shooting brings a handsome, injured stranger to her doorstep. Soon she's embroiled in human smuggling and kidnapping, while trying to resist the handsome government agent who challenges her at every step.

Ryder McKay—Member of a top secret commando group (SDDU), Ryder would like nothing more than to send Grace packing. She's in danger and she's in the way. But the stubborn beauty teaches him the meaning of courage, and soon becomes key to his investigation.

Esperanza Molinero—Her husband and children disappeared on the U.S. side of the border. She will do anything to find them.

Dylan Rogers—An old friend who rents the Cordero ranch. His main concern is Grace's safety. Or does he have other reasons for wanting her to return to the city?

Mikey Metzner—His company is suspected of hiring illegal immigrants. But how deep are they involved in human trafficking? Is he guilty, or just an easy target because he's the town's richest man?

SDDU—Special Designation Defense Unit. A top secret commando team established to fight terrorism and other international crime that affects the U.S. Its existence is known only by a select few. Members are recruited from the best of the best.

Colonel Wilson—Ryder's boss. He's the leader of the SDDU, reporting straight to the Homeland Security Secretary.

Chapter One

Ryder McKay leaned his back against the rough bark of a tree in the middle of a sparse South Texas mesquite grove, surrounded by darkness and silence. He'd been shot before. But this time it didn't look as if he would be walking away. He figured he had about another ten minutes to live.

He pressed his blood-crusted hands onto the gaping bullet wound in his thigh. If he let go to push himself to standing, he would bleed out on the spot. No point in standing, anyway. He wasn't going to make the long mile to where his pickup waited.

He grabbed for his belt and unbuckled it as blood gushed from the wound. Black specs swam in front of his eyes within seconds. He had to slap his hands back on the injury long before he could have tugged off the holster, the Taser, phone clip and all the other stuff he carried.

The amount of blood he'd lost already... If he let go again, he'd pass out before he could make a tourniquet.

He needed another plan. He ignored the light-headedness, the sweat trickling down his neck and the ants crawling over his legs. *Think.* He didn't believe in failed missions. He believed in never conceding defeat until you were six feet under.

He had to come up with a solution, and he had to do it on his own. Nobody at the new SDDU Texas satellite office knew where he was. When he'd driven off, he'd simply told Mo that he would be checking the border. He hadn't meant to come this far.

Normally, a dozen or so people worked at the Special Designation Defense Unit's Texas satellite office. Half of the top secret commando team was currently off on various missions in South America. Ryder and five others were on location here to address credible intelligence that a South-American drug lord had sold both weapons and smuggling services to a terrorist organization that planned on infiltrating the U.S.

The smugglers would cross at this section of the border—within a fifty-mile stretch—sometime next month. The recon team's job was to know the border area inside out by then—know the trails, know the players, and find assets who would be able to pass on useful information.

The rest of the team would be returning as their missions ended. Together, they would take out those terrorist the second the bastards set foot on U.S. soil.

He wanted to live long enough to be there for the takedown. Except, when his teammates realized he'd gone missing, hours from now, they would have a thousand acres to search. And a search like that could take days.

He only had minutes.

He gritted his teeth, casting a dark look at his cell phone that lay in pieces on the rocks a few hundred feet away where he'd first fallen.

He could have used his flashlight to signal for help, but, for that, too, he'd have to let the pressure off the wound. And nobody was around, anyway, in the middle of the abandoned South Texas borderlands. The light might even bring back the drug traffickers who'd shot him.

He hadn't squeezed off any shots into the air for the same reason.

He knew of only one ranch close enough so if someone was there, they might hear—but the one time he'd checked, the old house had looked abandoned. Nothing else for miles around but dust and heat.

He looked up to the sky, wondering if he had enough time to confess all his sins. Not a single star showed, nor the moon. A dark storm was gathering.

GRACE CORDERO SAT BACK in her grandfather's old recliner and rubbed her fingers over a spot of dirt on her jeans. She'd spent most of the day walking around the ranch, then cleaning the house to make her stay a little nicer.

"I don't like the idea of you out here alone." Dylan put his feet on the coffee table, work boots and all. The pose seemed relaxed, but the muscles around his eyes were drawn tight, and tension stiffened his shoulders. He had a number of businesses, at least two dozen employees, the kind of stuff that came with a lot of headaches.

She frowned at the boots on the table, but didn't tell him to mind his manners. He rented the ranch from her so technically he had a right to do whatever he pleased, even if he never used the house, just the land.

He watched her with those pale blue eyes she'd writ-

ten poems about back in high school. She'd been pitifully smitten. Now she could barely remember that
carefree, always-grinning-like-an-idiot teenage girl
she'd once been, let alone relate to her.

"Why don't you go over to Molly's? She loves you
to pieces."

Warmth spread through her. "I'll stop by." She loved
Molly, too. Dylan's sister had been her best friend back
in the day. But social visits would have to wait. She
looked through the window for a second, into the blind
night. "I came here for a reason."

He gave a slow nod, casting a sideways glance toward the brass urn on the fieldstone mantel above the
ornate fireplace her great-great grandfather had built.
"I want to go with you when… You know."

He wanted to be with her when she finally spread her
brother's ashes on the ranch, as Tommy had requested
during his long, losing battle to live.

"I appreciate that, Dylan. I do." She tried to think of
a way to say the rest without offending him. "But I'd
rather do it alone. I'm just still not at peace with this."
She wasn't at peace with a lot of things. Unease and
anxiety were her ruling emotions these days, along with
a good dose of anger and resentment.

"Of course." Dylan reached for her hand. "You take
whatever time you need."

A faint clap sounded in the distance, almost like a
gunshot. She pulled her hand away. "What was that?"

"Probably thunder. A storm is moving in." He looked
around the living room. "You cleaned."

"I hope to stay a couple of days."

A frown creased his forehead, then disappeared the

next second. "You know you can stay with us. Molly would love to have you."

She gave a tired smile as she shook her head. She needed time alone.

"Then stay at my place in Hullett." He kept an apartment in town, a two-bedroom bachelor pad where he took his dates. Molly was a single mom with an impressionable eight-year-old. And Dylan liked to keep his private business private, anyway.

She thought she saw a glint in his eyes, some emotion she couldn't identify. Was he remembering how it had been between them more than a decade ago? They did have good times.

Seemed as if a lifetime had passed since. The hotshot young football player had grown into an attractive man. A successful man. His pale blue eyes watched her with interest.

"How is business?" she asked to change the subject and the train of her thoughts. "I hope the ranch is good to you."

She and her brother had inherited the place after their grandfather's death. Tommy's illness had been bad enough by then that he'd had to leave the army. But he'd still had enough left in him to work the land for a couple of years before he had to move into Edinburg, closer to medical care, and then around the clock help toward the end.

Dylan renting the place was a tremendous relief. She needed the income to pay the taxes on the property, plus Tommy's medical bills. She'd even wondered, at times, if Dylan only rented because he knew she needed the money. Maybe it was his way of helping. For old time's sake.

"Business is fine," he said, with a look that told her he wasn't done with trying to talk her out of her solitude yet.

"I drove around when I got in. Doesn't look like you have any crops planted." It didn't look as if he'd planted anything last year, either. The land hadn't been worked in a while, scraggy weeds taking over the endless fields.

"Can't make a living from farming anymore." A hint of sadness settled on his face. "I have a deal with a company who does corporate retreats here. Survival training for business managers, a team building thing—they come from all over the country. They sleep in tents, learn how to get from point A to point B without GPS, deal with the elements, make their own food over an open fire. They even climb up and down the ravine."

Unease flashed through her at the thought of the steep ravine on the remote south edge of the property. "Somebody could get hurt."

"They're fully insured. They rappel up and down in hundred-degree heat, lose a couple of pounds and pay me a load of money for setting it all up, clearing bush when needed and trucking in supplies."

He grinned, and she could suddenly see the old Dylan in that smile. A wave of nostalgia hit her, for a time when everything was so much simpler, a time when she still had Gramps and Tommy.

The dull, ever-present ache in her chest intensified. *Think of something else.*

"I hope they're not hunting." She'd spent considerable time years ago posting signs to make sure everyone knew that absolutely no hunting was allowed on the property. She had a safe-haven agreement with Wildlife Protection. The ranch included over two hundred acres of dense brushland that gave home to some oce-lots, a highly endangered species slowly disappearing from South Texas.

She liked the idea of saving them. Saving something. She sure hadn't been able to save her grandfather or Tommy.

"They wouldn't know what to do with a rifle. Bunch of city slickers. But the trainers like to keep that sense of isolation for them, to better develop interdependence or whatever. So if you wouldn't mind…"

"I won't go anywhere near the ravine." She wouldn't have, anyway. She had a nice meadow picked for Tommy's ashes, not far from the house, a place where her brother had taught her horseback riding back in the day. *Good memories*. Focusing on those was the key.

Dylan settled deeper into the couch, apparently comfortable. "My offer to buy the ranch still stands."

A fine offer. And she had no intention of moving back here. Yet something held her back from agreeing to the sale. "I'm thinking about it."

"Good." He gave a quick smile. "How is work?"

"Busy."

She perched on the edge of her chair and felt guilty for wishing him gone. He'd always been a good friend to her, but she wanted to be alone tonight, her first night back.

"You got your own practice yet?"

"Almost." She put a smile on her face. "I have my last batch of veterinary exams coming up soon." For which she'd brought some books. Not that she had it in her to drag them out tonight.

"Could have gone to med school with the same effort

and be a human doctor. Pays better. You were a medic in the army. You already know half the stuff."

"Couldn't afford med school if I sold both my kidneys." And the truth was she couldn't handle any more people dying in her arms.

A yawn stretched her face against her will. "Sorry. I spent most of the day driving and walking around. I guess I'm not used to all this good country air anymore."

"A shame," he said as he stood, taking the hint. "Come back to Hullett with me. At least I have a working air conditioner."

"Thanks, but I'm fine here. Really."

He opened his mouth but was distracted by a mangy old cat that padded forward cautiously from the laundry room.

"Came scratching at the door as soon as I arrived," she said, maybe a little too defensively. "Might be one of the descendants of Gramps's batch of barn cats. I'll find her a good home before I go. You don't have to worry about her." The cat had had some badly infected thorns in her hind leg, which she'd taken care of already.

"You know why they call them barn cats, right? Because they're supposed to stay in the barn." He shook his head with a look that said he thought she was hopeless. "Whatever you do, don't name her."

She would leave that honor to whoever was going to take the cat. "I've managed to resist."

He looked skeptical.

"Say hi to Molly for me. I'll stop in to see her, I promise."

She walked him to the door, where he hesitated for a second before giving her a quick hug. She hugged him back then watched him walk to his brand-new Chevy truck, glanced up at the clouds that were rushing in to block out the moon. She hoped he'd get home before the storm hit.

The cat meowed behind her, but didn't step a foot outside. She didn't seem to want to get too far from the bowl of milk in the kitchen. Grace passed by her then closed the door and went around turning off the lights, alone at last in the old house that brought back way too many memories.

"Focus on the good," she told the cat, but meant the words for herself.

She picked up a box of Twinkie snacks from the counter, something she'd grabbed at the last gas station she'd stopped at on her way here. "Straight to the hips," she said to the cat as she opened the box.

She had the Twinkie halfway to her mouth when another clap in the distance stopped her. This time, she recognized the sound.

The gunshot came from the vicinity of the mesquite grove behind the fields.

Maybe she had a lost hiker on her land, or a bird-watcher—it had happened before. Then another shot came quickly, and another. Nine altogether.

Bam. Bam. Bam. Pause. *Bam.* Pause. *Bam.* Pause *Bam.* Pause. *Bam. Bam. Bam.*

Morse code or coincidence? If it was Morse code, the pattern spelled SOS.

Getting in trouble was easy around here, what with the snakes and the heat and other hazards of the land. And with the storm coming… Nobody should get stuck out there in that kind of weather. She set the Twinkie back in the box and put a bowl over it upside down on the counter so it wouldn't tempt the cat. Comfort food would have to wait. She'd need both hands for driving in the dark.

She hurried back to the front door and stepped into her boots, made sure she had her cell phone in her pocket and grabbed the industrial-strength flashlight from the peg. On second thought, she grabbed her grandfather's old hunting rifle, as well, along with a handful of bullets, then rushed to her car as the first raindrops splashed to the ground.

The paved road that led to town snaked in the opposite direction from where she was headed. She took the dirt road to the fields, beyond which lay sparse woods and brush and grassland—God's best country.

Darkness surrounded her, nothing visible beyond the path the headlights illuminated as the pickup rattled over the uneven ground. She wasn't scared, not on her grandfather's land. *Her land.* She knew every acre of it, had driven over it, ridden over it.

The road soon turned into an overgrown trail, bushes scratching against the side of the pickup. She pushed through and came to an open area, rattled over the dry clumps of grass. She slowed for two dry creek beds, then took the bumpy ride across them. It hadn't rained in forever. According to Dylan, just the week before, they'd had a pretty bad dust storm.

When she reached the spot she thought the shots had come from, she drove around in expanding circles, then continued on foot when the pickup could no longer handle the terrain. The flashlight found a pair of armadillos out on a date, but no humans. She loaded the rifle and squeezed a shot into the air.

A full year had passed since the last time she'd pulled

a trigger. Tension settled into her shoulders, pulling her muscles tight.

The shot reverberated in the silence of the night. Then another shot answered. Her heart rate picked up as she ran that way. Her palms were sweating. The trembling came. Then the flashbacks—of other dark nights, other shots, blood and pain, people dying. She kept on running.

After a few hundred feet or so, she could see a pinpoint of light in the distance, a flashlight that led her to a barely conscious man.

For a terrifying second, she was still on a battlefield, her mind unable to distinguish between past and present. Then the gruesome images slowly faded and she came back to reality, to the man lying on the ground in front of her.

"Are you okay?"

In his early thirties, he wore black cargo pants covered in blood, a black T-shirt and military-issue boots. She would have taken him for a border agent, but he didn't wear their insignia.

Not a local, either. She'd known most everyone around these parts at one point. He was about her age, so if he'd grown up here, they would have gone to the small school together in Hullett. She would have recognized him, despite the smudges of blood that covered his features.

Probably not one of Dylan's businessmen, unless he was their trainer. The stuff on his belt was all professional grade and then some. Question was, what was he doing here all alone, so far from the ravine? She took his gun and tucked it into her waistband behind her back, out of his reach. Probably an unnecessary precaution. He didn't look ready to reach for anything.

"What happened? What's your name?"

His eyes fluttered open, then closed again. He was only semiconscious, but he kept his hands pressed tight against a wound on his thigh. Smart man—he was focusing his energies where it most counted. She held the flashlight closer.

Gunshot wound. The bullet had gone in the back and came out the front. Definitely not a self-inflicted, accidental injury.

Keeping her rifle close at hand, she slipped off his belt and made a quick tourniquet. Then she ran back to her pickup, grabbed a half-empty water bottle that was still warm from the day's heat. It'd do in a pinch. She shook him so he'd revive enough to drink. He needed to replenish his fluids.

He needed an IV, but he wouldn't get that here.

When she had done all she could, she dialed 911. She didn't get through, of course—no reception. Cell phone coverage was spotty out here on a good day. With the storm moving in, the bars on her display were flatlining.

"Help." The single word slipped in a rasp whisper from the man's lips.

And when she looked up, his eyes were open again. She couldn't see their color in the dark, only that they were disoriented. "I'm trying."

He was a big man but, like her brother, she'd served in the United States Army and had gotten the best possible training. She bent and worked the guy's arm over her shoulder, supported his body weight as she struggled forward and dragged him toward the truck.

The rain had been picking up steadily, turning into a

downpour. Her feet slipped in the mud, but she wouldn't allow herself to stop, wouldn't allow him to slide to the ground. If he did, she might not be able to pick him up again.

She peered through the rain into the darkness, making sure she kept aware of her surroundings and didn't let him claim all of her attention. *Hurry.* Her rifle hung over her shoulder, his gun tucked behind her back, no way for her to quickly reach for either if whoever had shot him came back and caught her by surprise.

Lightning lit up the sky. The water was coming down in sheets by the time she reached her pickup. She dumped him in the passenger seat then ran around and jumped behind the wheel. The dry creek beds could fill quickly in weather like this. Then they'd both be trapped out here.

He coughed and opened his eyes as she drove way too fast over the uneven road, the pickup rattling.

"Can you tell me your name?"

"Ryder... McKay."

She didn't know any McKays around here. "Do you know who shot you?"

He passed out again before he could have answered.

Hot anger hit her, a hard punch right in the chest. This was her land, dammit. Stuff like this wasn't supposed to happen here.

The creek beds were filling up, but she made her way across them. The mud proved more dangerous, at the end. The pickup's tires spun out on a steep incline she tackled. Long minutes went wasted before she could maneuver the truck free.

"Hang in there," she murmured, not knowing which one of them she meant to bolster.

Her windshield wipers swished back and forth madly and still weren't enough. Intermittent lightning flashed across the landscape. The thunder sounded like heavy shelling. The ground shook as if bombs were falling. *Not now.* She bit her lip hard and used the sharp pain to yank herself back from the edge.

She navigated the barely visible road, doing her best to pay attention to everything at once: the mud, the injured man, the trees that could be hiding the shooter.

The drive back to the house took three times as long as the drive out. "Okay, we're here. You'll feel better once you're flat on your back and we're out of this rain."

She parked by the front door and dragged the man in, ignoring the mud they tracked all over the floor. A particularly nasty bolt of lightning drew her gaze to the window, and for a second she could see all that driving rain drowning the open land, field after field. No other houses.

Neighbors would be nice. The kind of close neighbors you could run over to in a time of need. But the ranch was in an isolated spot, the farthest house from town.

"Here we go." The old couch groaned under the man's weight as she laid him down. "I'll be back in a second."

She dashed back to the truck for her rifle and the veterinary supply bag behind her seat. She locked the front door on her way back in, something her grandfather hadn't done once in his life. They lived in good country, around good folks, he used to tell her.

She wondered what he would think about this. He'd have words to say. And not the kind of words you'd find in a church bulletin.

She wiped her face. No time to dry herself fully. *Bag. Scissors.* She cut off the man's pants so she could do a better job at assessing and cleaning his injury. If being a field medic in the army had taught her anything, it was to be resourceful and find a way to use whatever she had at her disposal. The veterinary bag was a godsend.

"Wake up. Can you hear me?"

No response. He didn't even flinch.

Clean the wound. Stop the bleeding. Dress the wound. Make him drink so he had enough fluids in him to get his blood pressure back up enough for him to permanently regain consciousness.

"You're going to make it. That's not a suggestion. That's an order." She snapped the same words at him as she had at soldiers on the battlefield.

She checked his limbs—everything moved, nothing felt broken. His heart beat slowly but steadily. His pupils were the same size, responding to light. His airways were open. He was in top combat shape, a big point in his favor. The patient's physical condition always had a big impact on recovery.

Once she finished with the basics, she moved to the niceties. She washed his bloody hands, then wiped his face with a wet washcloth. She'd definitely never met him before. In the light of the lamp and without the smudges on his face, she could fully see him at last: tussled dirty blond hair, straight nose, a masculine jaw, sexy lips. The fact that he looked drawn failed to deduct from how ridiculously handsome he was.

"Ryder McKay," she said his name out loud, then felt foolish when the cat padded in and gave her a curious look.

The scrawny feline assessed the situation while she licked her lips.

"That better not be cream on your whiskers," Grace warned the cat, pretty much resigning herself to the fact that her Twinkie was history. "And you better not get sick from all that sugar. I'm not kidding."

The cat flashed her a superior look then strolled away.

The man's eyes blinked open slowly, the color of desert honey, then closed again.

"Ryder? You need to wake up. Can you hear me?"

He didn't stir, not even when a loud banging shook the front door the next second.

Grace jumped to her feet, faced the door in a fight-ready stance, her heart lurching into a race before she caught herself. *It's not an attack. Someone's just stopping by for a visit. Most likely.*

Could be Dylan. She walked to the window, but could see only her own pickup in the driveway through the sheets of rain.

Looking sideways, she could just barely make out a shadow outside her door. Maybe Ryder McKay had a partner out there who was looking for shelter. She hurried to the door and put her hand on the key, but then hesitated. Whoever was outside could just as easily be the one who'd shot McKay.

She ran back to him and pulled the large afghan over his head, covering his entire body. The couch stood in line of sight from the front door. This way, at least he wouldn't be immediately seen.

The late-night visitor knocked again, even louder and more forcefully.

She strode back to the door, reached for her grandfather's rifle that she'd hung back up on the peg, then drew a deep breath. "Who is it?"

Chapter Two

The short, plump woman on the other side of the door stood soaked to the skin and poised to flee. She was unarmed and covered in mud—must have slipped a couple of times on her way here. She broke into rapid Spanish.

Grace put away the rifle and motioned her in. *"Yo no habla Español. Lo siento."*

She'd forgotten ninety percent of the Spanish she'd learned in high school. And the woman spoke way too fast to even catch individual words, anyway.

But one didn't have to be bilingual to understand that she was in trouble and ready to drop from exhaustion. Scratches covered her arms, dirt and leaves clung to her wet hair, dark circles rimmed her eyes. She rushed on with her torrent of unintelligible words.

Maybe her car had broken down somewhere. Nothing they could do about that until morning.

"Mañana, all right? We'll figure this out tomorrow. How about you take a nice hot shower and get some sleep?"

Grace motioned her to the stairs and kept her body between her and the sofa to block the woman's view of Ryder, barely covered by the afghan. Upstairs, she showed her to the bedroom she'd cleaned for herself earlier, pointing out the bathroom next door.

"Cómo te llamas?" She used one of the few expressions she remembered, as she pulled a dry T-shirt and sweatpants from the bag she'd brought and hadn't unpacked yet.

The woman put a hand to her chest. "Esperanza." Then she rushed on with plenty of things to say, unfortunately all in Spanish.

"Okay, Esperanza. *Me llamo Grace.*" She handed over the clothes. "Take it easy, get some rest." She pointed to the bed. "You're safe here."

Esperanza, barely strong enough to stand, stopped talking and nodded. Her shoulders slumped, tears gathered in her eyes. She looked pitifully, heart-twistingly dejected, but seemed to accept at last that they weren't going to understand each other. She moved to leave.

"No. You stay here. *Mañana,* we'll take care of everything. You can't go anywhere else tonight." Grace pointed at the rain lashing the window. *"Muy peligroso."* Very dangerous.

The woman paled, then nodded, the fight going out of her. She sank onto the bed.

"I'll bring you something to eat, okay?" Grace grabbed her bag then left the woman and padded downstairs.

She made two sandwiches for Esperanza and grabbed a bottle of water to take to her. The woman accepted the nourishment, setting everything on the bedcover next to her.

"Good night. *Buenas noches.* Everything will be better in the morning. You'll see. *Mañana.*" Grace gave a big thumbs-up.

But the woman didn't cheer up in the least. She looked heartbroken beyond words.

Grace went back downstairs and mopped up the mud, exhaustion settling into her bones. She didn't look forward to having to clean another bedroom before she could go to sleep. But by the time she changed into dry clothing and was ready to head back up the stairs, Ryder was blinking awake. She grabbed the chance and poured some orange juice into him.

"Are you with the team-building people?" In that case, she could call Dylan once her phone decided to work again, and he could get in touch with the rest of the guy's team. They had to be looking for him.

But after clearing his throat, the man said, "border protection," his voice hoarse and weak.

She winced, thinking of Esperanza upstairs who might or might not be from the local Hispanic community. Maybe she'd just sneaked across the border. Not something that normally happened on the ranch. The south side of the property was pretty inhospitable terrain, even discounting the impassable ravine. No shade, frequent brush fires, an endless walk and several families of ocelots in the brush were a pretty good deterrent.

There were easier places to cross, and most everybody knew it.

Yet, Esperanza *was* here.

And someone had shot Ryder.

Unfortunately, he passed out again before she could ask him any questions about that. Familiar anxiety, one that often stirred without warning these days, tightened her muscles. She worked her breathing to keep those muscles from locking up completely. *No big deal. Just an injured man.* She wasn't in the middle of full-out war or anything.

Rain pelted the windows as she looked into the man's pale face. He'd be gone, come morning. So would Esperanza. She would drive the woman into town where Esperanza could get back to her people or at least find someone who spoke Spanish.

Then she would take care of her brother's remains and go home, Grace decided, and making a decision— an escape plan—relaxed her a little. She'd planned on staying a couple of days, but the peace and solitude she'd come to seek had been shattered. She looked at the urn on the mantel.

"Nothing ever turns out the way you'd expect," she told Tommy, and missed his quiet, strong company suddenly with a sharp, heartrending pain.

RYDER WOKE TO THE SUN shining through the windows and had no idea where he was, which he found less than encouraging. His weapon was gone. Bad news number two. And he didn't have pants on, which added to his general sense of unease. He looked around the faded living room, at the old, rustic furnishings. He recognized them and the unique fireplace from when he'd peeked through the windows last week. He was at the ranch he'd thought abandoned.

Female voices captured his attention, an indistinct chatter. There were people in the house with him. Could be good news, or bad. He needed to face the music either way.

He drank the orange juice left on the rustic side table next to the sofa, then glanced under the bandage on his leg and noted the professional-looking stitches. Obviously, at one point he'd gotten medical help. Yet he didn't remember a trip to the hospital, or here.

Ignoring the pain, he quietly pushed to his feet and wrapped the pink-and-purple afghan around his waist— an indignity he couldn't find a way around. He turned to look for a weapon. *Yowza.*

Dizziness hit him so hard, he had to brace his hand against the back of the sofa. He moved slower as he stepped forward and grabbed the poker from the fireplace, then headed toward the voices.

Two women stood by the kitchen counter, trying to communicate, one in English, the other one in rushed Spanish. Neither noticed him. The Mexican woman looked drawn and scared; the tall, lean Texan seemed exasperated.

Neither was armed, so he leaned the poker against the wall before he stepped forward. Not so far, of course, that he couldn't easily reach back for the make-shift weapon.

All conversation stopped. Sharp tension filled the sudden silence as they turned to him.

He put a friendly smile on his face. "Ladies."

The Texan dashed for him on legs that went on forever. "You shouldn't be on your feet." She propped him up, then helped him to a chair by the table. Her dark auburn hair was chin-length, a stubborn wave curled under her ear. Emerald-green eyes shone from her face.

Something about her body pressed against his felt familiar. He had a sudden flashback of the two of them in the dark, in the rain.

"Here." She moved with purposeful efficiency as she settled him on the chair. Her soft hair tickled his jaw for a second before she pulled away. "Let me make you some eggs. You need the protein."

He needed a lot of things, his Beretta being at the top of the list. But it didn't seem polite to demand a handgun when someone just offered to feed you breakfast. "Where am I?"

"At the Cordero ranch. I'm Grace."

She was pretty in a simple sort of way—no overdone makeup or freaky hairdo—her look and gestures natural, if not completely relaxed. She had a lean body that clearly saw regular exercise. She kept casting wary glances his way. "Do you remember me bringing you back here?"

"Not exactly." He remembered running into smugglers who shot him. Then he remembered being on the brink of death, getting desperate enough to shoot his gun into the air, risking leading the smugglers back to him. The desperate act of a man who'd run out of choices.

But Grace had showed instead of the gunmen, apparently.

Must have been his lucky day.

Unless, of course, she was somehow connected to the smugglers. But then why would she save him? He decided to trust her for the time being, but moved his chair, anyway, so he'd be within reach of the knife on the counter.

A rough-looking cat appeared from nowhere and measured him up.

"Her name is Twinky," Grace said. "She's a stray."

The cat sauntered closer, rubbed herself against his legs, then sauntered away.

The Mexican woman kept wringing her hands and talking all through their exchange.

Grace shot him a helpless, reluctant look. "Do you know what she's saying?"

He asked her to slow down a little and focused on the flood of words. "She's looking for her husband and her kids. Five-year-old twins, a boy and a girl."

Grace paled, her gaze flying to the window. "They were out there last night with her?"

He repeated the question in Spanish, then translated for Grace.

"They came to the U.S. with her husband two months ago."

He asked a couple more questions and got the rest of the story. Didn't much like it.

"Her husband got a visa to come and work for the wire mill in Hullett. The whole family was supposed to get papers, but something delayed hers at the last minute. The company representative told her she had to stay behind for a few days, and then she could come after her family once everything was straightened out."

The woman was clearly distraught and desperate, wringing her hands as she waited for him to finish translating. He didn't think she was lying.

Grace brought him another glass of orange juice, then got a carton of eggs out of the fridge, her attention on him as he continued to translate.

"She was told the children should go ahead with the husband. School was starting. The representative even got them fully loaded backpacks and everything."

His instincts prickled. He asked a few more questions.

"She says she last saw her family when they crossed

the border. Never heard from them again. Never heard from the company representative. She can't reach him at the phone number he'd given her. She talked to the Mexican police. She even called the Hullett police here. Neither would help her."

Grace turned on the stove under the eggs then put a hand on the younger woman's shoulder. The small, sympathetic gesture made tears gather in the woman's eyes all over again.

"Did you come across the border last night with a guide?" he asked in Spanish, wanting as much detail as possible.

She hung her head, her shoulders tensing as she backed away from him. For a second he thought she might make a run for the door. Grace either understood some of his words or she'd guessed them because she positioned herself so she could block him if he made a move. That she thought he might give chase was flattering, but wholly impossible. He could barely put weight on his injured leg.

Then, peeking from behind Grace, the young woman gave a hesitant nod at last, and rushed to explain.

"She's afraid that something terrible happened to her family," he told Grace. "All she wants is to find them and make sure they're safe."

"I'll take her to town after breakfast and help her with the authorities," Grace said immediately. "If you could, please, tell her."

He shook his head. "When I call in and they come to pick me up, we're going to have to detain her. Other people will want to ask her questions, too. She's here without papers. She's not going to be let loose, no matter what her purpose is here."

And then it happened. In the blink of an eye, Grace Cordero morphed from a pretty hostess cooking for her guests into a stunning warrior amazon. The gentle, nurturing aura disappeared in a second. She pulled herself to full height and stalked right up to him, a steely expression coming onto her face.

Yowza. The budding interest his battered body had registered toward her earlier turned into instant, full-blown lust. Whatever blood he had left rushed south.

All right, then. Looked as if he was going to live, after all, he thought with some amusement and not a little surprise at his visceral response to her. It'd been a while since a woman made him sit up and take notice. He'd been too busy lately.

Her eyes flashed as she faced him down, her jaw tight, her shoulders stiffening. "She stays where she is." She didn't raise her voice, but the hard tone carried plenty of warning.

While she had a core of kindness, one that would push her out into a storm in the night to save a stranger, one that would have her take in a distraught woman without questions, she also had a whole other side. His instincts said it was a side a smart person wouldn't mess with. He had a feeling Grace Cordero would make a bad enemy.

"Do you live here?" he asked her in a mild tone to defuse the sudden tension.

"I arrived yesterday morning," were the words that came out of her mouth, but the flash in her eyes said: *none of your business.*

"How long are you staying?"

Her chin came up. "As long as it takes to help Esperanza."

And Ryder drew a slow breath. Grace wasn't staying. Not if he had anything to do with it. Her land wasn't safe now, and it would be even less so in the upcoming weeks. She needed to leave.

SOMETHING ABOUT THE UTTER devastation in Esperanza's eyes reached the grief in her own heart. She knew what it was like to lose family. She had nobody left.

Grace pulled her cell phone from her pocket and tossed it to Ryder. She'd done the best she could last night, but he still needed medical attention. "Call whoever you need, but leave me and Esperanza out of this."

The sooner he left, the better.

She'd meant to call first thing in the morning, but hadn't had the chance. She'd ended up sleeping in the recliner to keep an eye on him overnight. She'd woken to Esperanza coming downstairs, and drew the woman into the kitchen so they wouldn't wake Ryder. Of course, he woke up, anyway, a few minutes later.

Unconscious, he'd been manageable. Sitting at her kitchen table, he looked fairly intimidating. He was pale and weak, but obviously well-built, a fighting machine on his better days. He had a sharp gaze, a pronounced, masculine chin, straight nose and a mouth that awakened some secret feminine longing inside her.

Not to be acted upon, obviously.

"If you work for border patrol, why aren't you wearing their uniform?"

Esperanza watched, her face scrunched with worry, probably aware that her fate was being decided.

"I'm on a special team."

If he thought that would impress Grace, he had another think coming. "Can't say I trust government men as far as I can throw them."

He kept his face emotionless as he asked, "Any particular reason?"

She didn't mind telling him. All the anger was still there, simmering just under her skin.

"My brother was in the first Gulf War. Got sick. The government never acknowledged that he'd been exposed to biological weapons. We went through hell to get him proper health care." She was convinced that if Tommy had gotten better help earlier, he would be still alive today.

The thought tore open a barely scabbed over wound deep inside her.

"And here you are, a doctor, unable to help him. That must have been doubly frustrating."

She shot him a blank look.

He gestured toward his injured leg. "You put in some fine stiches."

"I was an army medic." And now almost a veterinarian. She could still save lives, and animals were so much less complicated than humans.

He looked at her through narrowed eyes, as if he was trying to puzzle her out. Good luck with that. These days her thoughts were such a tangled mess, she could barely make sense of them herself.

Nor could she make much sense of him, so far. Beyond his name, she still barely knew anything about him. Well, other than he was annoyingly hot.

Since he was strangely getting under her skin, she decided to go on the offensive. "What were you doing on my land?"

"That's classified information."

Of course it was. If she had a dollar for every time she'd heard that answer while trying to investigate just what chemicals Tommy had been exposed to…. She returned to the stove to remove the eggs from the fire.

He was dialing the phone behind her, but said very little beyond his location when the other end picked up. He was long done before she turned around with his breakfast. Maybe he'd be in a better mood to help once he was fed.

She split the eggs between him and Esperanza, who ate quickly, standing by the counter. She didn't seem to want to go anywhere near the table and Ryder. Grace couldn't blame her. Even in a weakened state, the man was pretty intimidating.

"Much appreciated," he said and dug in. Whether he was hungry or simply ate because he knew he needed the energy, he did a fair amount of damage in a short time.

Grace watched him for a minute or so, wanting to give him time to eat in peace, but she ran out of patience too quickly. "Esperanza needs to find her family. I want to help her."

"The authorities will help her," he said between two bites, then spoke to Esperanza briefly in Spanish.

Tears rolled down the woman's face as she set her empty plate in the sink. She looked as if she'd just been told that she'd be taken out back and shot.

"The authorities have done nothing to help her until now," Grace argued, frustration humming through her. She hadn't been able to help her brother, but she *could* help Esperanza. If Ryder didn't stand in her way.

He finished his eggs, leaned back in his chair and watched her for a few seconds. Then his face hardened suddenly. "How long have you been aware that you have drug smuggling and human trafficking on your land?"

The air got stuck in her lungs. "We never had any of that out here." Of course, she hadn't lived here for years. Still, Tommy hadn't mentioned anything. Neither had Dylan.

But Ryder had gotten shot. Had he been confronting drug runners? And Esperanza *was* here. What if all this was just the tip of the iceberg?

"Were you shot by smugglers?" Not that she was ready to believe that, but she couldn't pretend that it had been a hunting accident, either. She'd known from the beginning that it had been something a lot more sinister; she just hadn't wanted to acknowledge it. She sank into the chair across the table from him.

She'd come to spread her brother's ashes in the most peaceful, nicest place on earth, in accordance with his wishes. But suddenly, the ranch seemed a much more dangerous place than she'd remembered.

"I can't comment on an ongoing investigation."

God forbid someone told her what was going on on *her* land. But instead of pushing for an answer about that, she decided to pick her battles. "Esperanza had nothing to do with whatever happened to you. We both know she didn't shoot you. How about you give her a break?"

"I can't."

"You could pretend you never saw her. I could have just hidden her upstairs until you were gone." In hindsight, not doing just that had been incredibly stupid. They could have avoided all of this.

"I don't play those kinds of games."

No, he probably didn't. He looked as serious as a longhorn stampede.

"Don't you have a heart?" The words burst from her in a fit of frustration.

"I'm going to take her into custody," Ryder said in a tone that bore no argument. "We'll consider it a voluntary surrender. I might be able to arrange for her record not to be marked, so she'll be able to get an actual visa and come back legally as soon as that's processed."

"And who's going to look for her husband and children?" she challenged.

He measured Esperanza up, then turned his attention to Grace. "I will. I'm interested in criminal activity in the area. Her family's disappearance could be connected to the case I'm investigating."

"Which is?"

"A matter of national security."

She could have cheerfully strangled the man. "Whatever happens on my land concerns me."

"The concerns of private citizens are secondary in this case."

Words easily said. And easily abused.

And what if he didn't follow through? If he found that there was no connection, after all, he'd probably drop the search in a second. She could all too easily see the kids and the husband becoming yet other victims the system failed.

She leaned forward in her seat. "I can help you. I've been living in Bryan for the past few years, but I know this area. I know the people around here."

He pinned her with a hard look, suddenly appearing stronger than he had a minute ago. "Not only won't you involve yourself in this, you won't talk about it, either. To anyone. You never saw me. I was never here. Is that clear?"

The strength of his voice surprised her, gave her a glimpse of what he might be like when he wasn't way-laid by massive blood loss. *Tough and stubborn.* She gritted her teeth, fighting the urge to upend the egg plate over his head.

But he distracted her with, "I don't suppose you have a spare pair of men's pants."

She was tempted to leave him in the pink-purple af-ghan her grandmother had crocheted, just to spite him. But she didn't want to risk the afghan slipping as he got up. So she shot him a glare and stomped up to Tommy's bedroom, grabbed the rattiest, most ridiculous-looking farmer's overalls out of the closet and brought them down. The man needed something loose. Tommy's jeans would have never fit over his bandages.

He lifted an eyebrow, but didn't say anything, just took the denim and shuffled into the laundry room that opened off the kitchen. She tried not to stare when he came out. The overalls ended above his ankles, since Tommy had been shorter. His dirty-blond hair stuck up in every direction, his face pale.

And the bastard still managed to look sexy. It was the lips, she decided, and turned from him as the sound of arriving vehicles filtered in from the outside. She strode to the door and yanked it open to glare at the men, presumably Ryder's buddies who'd come to take him and Esperanza away.

She lost her breath for a second.

Oh, sweet heaven. For real?

The men who strategically exited the dark SUVs—all combat ready—wore the same black commando gear

Ryder had had on when she'd found him. They were all built, moving with grace, radiating strength. They were so hot, all five of them, that they could have had their own pinup calendar.

If it weren't for the all too real we-mean-business look in their eyes and their authentic arsenal of weapons, she would have thought that they were hot stuff actors hired to play a commando team in some top budget movie.

They looked her over, some with suspicion, some with appreciation, and honest to goodness made her feel flustered. No small feat, considering that during her military career she'd been surrounded by thousands of horny men.

"Ma'am," said the tall, Viking-looking one with the reddish-blond hair. "We're here for a friend of ours."

He didn't introduce himself, nor did he refer to Ryder by name. She itched to know just what kind of an op they were running.

"In there." She jerked her head, hating the way the morning was turning out. She might have been able to stand up against Ryder in regards to Esperanza, but no way could she stand up against the six of them.

Game over.

She watched as they tried hard not to laugh at Ryder's appearance in the overalls. But there was a lot of smirking going on as they helped him to the door.

He stopped in the threshold. "I appreciate the help, Grace."

She didn't say *you're welcome,* just stood there with her arms crossed.

"I had a gun," he said then.

Fine. She stepped to the hall table and pulled open the top drawer, then handed him his gun belt.

He left with a nod, followed by one of his buddies—built like a tank—who was escorting Esperanza. Half of the man's left eyebrow was missing, giving him a fierce appearance. Esperanza looked about ready to faint.

The rest of the men inspected Grace's living room as if they were undecided whether to leave or pull out a search warrant.

Twinky padded in from the direction of the kitchen; the Viking gave her a careful look.

Grace rolled her eyes. "What? You want to frisk the cat?"

The man's startling blue eyes cut to her and he coughed. His face remained impassive, but he might have been trying to cover up a laugh. The others strode out and he walked after them.

She followed after Esperanza and gave the crying woman a hug. *"Lo siento,"* she whispered into her ear. *I'm sorry.* "I will do whatever I can to help. I'm going to look for your family, okay?"

And maybe Esperanza understood, because she slipped a folded-up piece of paper into Grace's hands, careful so nobody would see the furtive maneuver, her red-rimmed eyes hanging on Grace's face, begging. She looked as miserable as a person could be, but followed the men without resisting. Then she disappeared in the back of one of the vehicles, no longer visible behind the tinted window.

"I do appreciate what you did for me," Ryder said again as he got into the passenger seat of the same vehicle.

Grace turned her back on him, marched inside the house, then slammed the door behind her.

Only then did she open the piece of paper.

Two little kids smiled at her from the photograph, a boy and a girl, their eyes laughing into the camera. Their parents stood behind them, a world of love in their eyes as they looked at their children. She turned the photo over. *Paco, Esperanza, Miguel y Rosita.*

Miguel was maybe two inches taller than his twin, his arms protectively around his little sister.

She had a picture in that same pose with Tommy, although the age difference had been bigger between them.

She glanced at the brass urn on the mantel and her heart constricted.

What if Ryder didn't fulfill his promise?

Children, even American children, fell through the cracks every single day. What if nobody went to look for Rosita and Miguel?

She squared her shoulders. *Somebody would,* she decided.

Chapter Three

Ryder took notes at the SDDU's new satellite site as Esperanza Molinero repeated her story. Raymund, better known as Ray, Armstrong, sat with them. The two of them were senior team members, based on length of service in the SDDU. The rest of the men busied themselves elsewhere so as not to overwhelm her and make her feel threatened.

"Did the guide bring a whole group or you alone?" he asked in Spanish.

"I sold my wedding ring so he would bring me. I came alone. I sold my bicycle and our furniture. Even the kitchen table Paco made me as a wedding gift. Where will my Paco eat when he comes home?"

Ray exchanged a look with Ryder that said he didn't expect that issue to come up. Something Ryder had considered, as well. The man should have called his wife by now, got word back to her. If he hadn't, he was possibly dead, or in some other bad trouble.

"Was your husband a drug mule? Did anyone give him any suspicious packages to take to the U.S. with him?" Ray asked, sliding lower in his chair, trying to look as small and nonthreatening as he could, a challenge for a big chunk of Viking like him. The blood of his marauding ancestors ran thick in his veins, there was no mistaking it. Mostly, it was an advantage, but not today. Esperanza eyed him warily.

Fresh tears welled in her eyes. "My Paco was a good man. An honest man."

"The kids were given backpacks of school supplies from the so-called company representative," Ryder put in, repeating what she'd told him at the ranch.

Ray asked Esperanza about that; she insisted that the bags contained nothing but notebooks and pencils. She looked confused, probably not understanding why they were asking her about the bags instead of her kids.

"Of course, she wouldn't have checked the padding," Ray said in English.

Ryder nodded. *Exactly.*

"You're sure about his name?" He wanted to get back to the human trafficking. The same man who brought her over might be the guide for the terrorists, in the not-too-distant future.

"Dave," the woman said then struggled with the next word. "Snebl."

"Where did you cross?"

"I couldn't see in the dark. We walked for a long time together. When he saw the storm, he said he was leaving. I gave him everything I had, all the rest of my money, my bag. But he turned around. He told me to keep walking."

She was lucky he didn't hurt her. Robbing people who came across the border was a common racket. If their guide didn't do it, then one of the groups who made a living from robbing illegal immigrants did. The men and women usually brought their most valuable possessions with them to start a new life. The hits could be lucrative, and the victims couldn't turn to the police, so the robbers nearly always got away with it.

Ryder shifted in his seat. His job was to defend his country and if he saw anyone breaking the law, do something about it. Either you broke the law or you didn't. He preferred to look at things in black-and-white. He hated shades of gray.

He was a soldier. He got a command, he carried it out. There was no evaluation of the mission, no second-guessing his superior officer. That was how the army, where he'd started out, worked, as did his current team the SDDU, Special Designation Defense Unit, a top secret commando team.

But nothing seemed clear-cut here. The land along the border was its own universe. Some of the people he'd met were clearly criminals, others victims, some both at the same time. Motivations were complicated.

He thought of Grace Cordero—the definition of *complicated*. A smart man would leave that attractive bundle of trouble well alone. Like he was going to do. To get a good head start, he put Grace from his mind and focused on the woman in front of him.

"Please," she begged them. "Help me."

He did feel sorry for Esperanza. She didn't cross the border with criminal intent, she didn't want to stay and live off taxpayer's money. She was looking for her husband and children because the authorities had failed her.

Yet, what she'd done *was* illegal.

He had no choice but to take her to border patrol and send her back home. No choice at all, even if a sharp-eyed beauty called Grace Cordero would hate him for it.

She didn't believe in the system.

He did. He'd sworn to defend it.

"Doesn't make any sense, if you ask me," Ray said in English. "The Cordero ranch isn't a known smuggling corridor. The terrain is too rough. There are easier points for crossing."

Yet the man who'd shot him had been out there. Ryder smoothed his black cargo pants over the bandages on his thigh. He'd been to the emergency room and back, the wound had been disinfected again, his stitches inspected and pronounced exemplary.

He'd been forced to lie down while they'd dripped a full bag of IV fluids into him, and had plenty of time to think. Maybe the spot had been chosen specifically because the smugglers thought nobody would be looking there.

He listened as Ray asked Esperanza some of the same questions she'd already answered, wording them differently this time to see if he could trip her. But she stayed consistent. Nothing indicated that she was lying.

They had alerted border patrol to her presence, but not to the shooting. Their operation was top secret, dealing with a terror threat. His small team had come to the area on the pretense that they were surveying border traffic for a new proposal for increased funding for CBP, Customs and Border Protection.

They were more than a match for their enemies, the special team consisting of trained and experienced commandos who did this for a living. As much as they respected the work CBP did, several recent busts had proven that not all the border agents could be trusted. Some were on the take from the traffickers.

And this was one mission where Ryder's team couldn't take any chances.

"I was cold because I had to swim," Esperanza was saying.

"Rio Grande." Ray looked at Ryder. "Can't believe she made it. The current can be a killer in places. Add the darkness and that storm." He shook his head.

"I was scared that the water would rise to the ceiling and I would drown," she said, not having understood the two men's exchange in English.

Ceiling? Then it all made sense suddenly.

"Tunnel," Ray and he said at the same time. Now at least they knew what they had to be looking for when they were out there scouring the land day after day. All that water from the rain had been running down and filling a tunnel.

"Do you remember anything about where you came out? In brush? Trees? Open fields?"

"In a ditch. I couldn't see much in the dark and the rain."

And no matter how hard they pressed her after that, she couldn't give them any further information. So Ryder escorted the woman to the crossing point, talked to the guards and walked her across. They had her contact information, the village she lived in and the phone number of her priest, since her house didn't have a phone line.

"Don't come back," he told her. "It's not safe. Your children need a mother. You stay here, and I'll go and look for them, all right?" he said in Spanish, and handed her enough money to get her to her village.

Tears streamed down her face. "Paco loves me. He wouldn't leave me. He wouldn't take my babies. He would die for me. I would die for him."

"I believe you." He spoke the truth. He believed in

that kind of love between a man and a woman, even if he'd never experienced it himself. His parents had that.

He left her and walked back across to his car, feeling somehow guilty and inadequate, even if he was doing the right thing.

A text message with photo pinged onto his phone as he started the engine—a blue-eyed newborn with a pink ribbon in her hair. A birth announcement from Mitch Mendoza. Ryder grinned, happy for his friend, but he also felt a sense of longing. He wanted what Mitch had—his true mate, the one that could make him happy.

He wanted a partner like Mitch had found, someone who would fight by his side and go with him on missions, someone to have his back during the day and fill his arms at night. Mitch had been over-the-moon happy since he'd met Megan. The couple was assigned to the SDDU's Texas office, but were on leave at the moment for the birth of their baby.

They had something Ryder had never had before. And he couldn't help but want a taste of it.

He'd been thinking about a wife lately. Kids.

A call interrupted that warm little fantasy.

"Shep and Mo are heading back," Ray said. "I'm about to leave for the Cordero ranch to look for the tunnel with the others. Jamie says last night's rain washed away all the tracks. I don't see how we can find the damned thing unless we stumble on it by accident. The report on Grace Cordero came in after you left, by the way. Squeaky clean. She has a hell of a service record. She did two tours of duty in Iraq. Are you coming out here?"

"I'm heading into Hullett to talk with the sheriff.

Want to see if he has any information on Paco Molinero and those kids."

"They came through with visas. I don't think Paco could give us much on the human trafficking."

A good point, but Ryder wanted Grace Cordero packed up and gone, and the quickest way to achieve that was to close the Molinero case as expediently as possible by finding Esperanza's family for her.

Then Grace would go back to where she'd come from and his team would have free rein over her ranch. He didn't like the idea of her out there alone, with criminal activity going on around her. She'd be unsafe and underfoot, a double negative.

He reached the next intersection and took the turn toward her ranch on impulse. But he found the driveway empty when he reached the house. His knock on the door went unanswered.

She'd better not be out there riding around the fields. He would have to warn her about that when he caught up with her. She needed to stay off the land until they figured out what was going on and found the damned tunnel.

He considered looking for her, but then he glanced at his watch and got back into his car. If he wanted to catch the sheriff at the office, he had to get going.

An hour later, he caught the man at his desk.

"So you're not with CBP?" Sheriff Denholtz ran his thumb over his considerable mustache. His large belly fairly stretched his uniform. His cowboy hat sat on the desk in front of him. He was in his mid-thirties, pretty young to make sheriff. But he acted as if he'd had the job for decades.

"I'm affiliated with CBP." Ryder gave his cover.

Since his team had no idea who they could trust around here, the rule of thumb was to trust no one. "I'm working on a special project."

"I thought the U.S. Customs and Borders Special Response Team handled those."

"You're right about that." People liked to hear that they were right. When you were trying to build rapport, it didn't hurt to say it. "This is different," he added. "My team is here to survey the border situation and make recommendations for policy makers."

"Strangers coming in, telling our local boys how to do their business." Denholtz pulled a toothpick from his shirt pocket and started chewing on it.

"I just need to have a list of Mexican nationals that ran into any kind of trouble here over the past two months."

The man drew his spine straight. "We don't have a smuggling problem in Hullett. I run a tight ship."

"No doubt, Sheriff. Still, if I could get that list."

The man sucked on the toothpick. "I'll tell one of my boys to get right on it. I'll have it faxed to CBP when it's ready."

"If you could fax it straight to me, it would be very helpful." He scribbled the office's fax number on the back of his fake card and slid it across the desk.

From the look the sheriff was giving him, he wouldn't hold his breath.

He resisted the urge to take a tougher tone. He needed to gain the local law's cooperation. If he pushed too hard, the sheriff might wonder if he had a special agenda, and his special agenda was top secret.

A deputy stuck his head in the door. "Gracie Cordero is here to see you, Sheriff."

Surprise flashed across the man's face, then a smile spread his mustache. He spit the toothpick into the garbage can and pushed to his feet.

Ryder gritted his teeth as the man passed by him without a word of apology for the interruption.

"Gracie, sweetheart. Ain't you a sight for sore eyes?" The words filtered through the door the sheriff had left open behind him.

"Good to see you, Shane. How is Mattie?"

"She's fine. Kids are so big you wouldn't recognize them. I heard about Tommy. I'm awful sorry about that. He was a real stand-up guy, your brother."

"He was." Grace's voice turned somber.

Ryder couldn't see her from where he was sitting, but he would recognize her voice anywhere. She had a melodious tone, not silky and seductive, yet still somehow sexy and feminine, except when she got herself all worked up and her voice turned hard and clipped.

"You back for good, then? Mattie would love that."

"For a week or two, at least. I'll stop in to see her and the kids."

"Anything I can help you with, sweetheart?"

Ryder rolled his eyes. Quite a bit different reception from the one he'd gotten.

"I'm looking for a guy by the name of Paco Molinero. He might have come to town with his two small kids, Miguel and Rosita."

"You hired someone for the ranch?"

"I know his wife in a roundabout way. He's gone missing."

"She ought to report that. I can send a deputy out to her house."

"She's on the other side of the border."

A moment of pause came. "You can file a missing person report, I suppose. You got the details?"

"Most of them. I also have a picture."

Ryder's ears perked up at that.

"Joey," the sheriff called out. "I want you to run this man through the system right now. Let's see if we get a hit."

"Yessir."

"How about a cup of coffee while we wait?" the sheriff offered next. "There might even be a couple of cookies left."

"Mattie's?" she asked in a kid's Christmas-morning voice.

Ryder stood and strode out, but all he could see was their disappearing backs as they walked down the hallway, chitchatting like two old friends. He decided to avoid the indignity of chasing after them.

She laughed and put her hand on the sheriff's shoulder as he said something amusing. Which annoyed Ryder more than it should have.

He wanted to go after them and demand the information he needed, but he had a feeling the sheriff would resist anyone who challenged his authority here, in his own little kingdom. So he strode out of the station, calling Shep, one of his teammates back at the office, for an update.

The news was less than encouraging. They couldn't find the tunnel.

"Any luck in Hullett?" Shep wanted to know.

"I'll get what I came for."

"Locals proving too difficult for you?"

"The usual small-town stuff."

"Maybe you'll find yourself a nice small-town girl."

Telling the guys that he was looking to settle down had clearly been a mistake. "Maybe you'll step on a rattler."

Shep laughed. "Come on now. What was her name again? Vivien?"

"Victoria." He bit out the single word. On a long night patrol with Shep, he'd unfortunately shared his vision of what he was looking for: tough, athletic, ready to go, a partner in fight as well as in the bedroom. Tough enough to survive his kind of life, but soft enough to be the mother of his children, basically.

He might have shared that he was partial to blondes with long hair, the longer the better. And since they'd been talking about her, it was easier to give her some sort of name, for convenience's sake. Not that he meant she had to be named Victoria, of course, which would be idiotic. But since then, even to himself, he'd begun to refer to this dream woman as Vicky.

GRACE TUCKED HER SHORT, dark bob behind her ears as she ran down the front stairs of the police station. She frowned at the man leaning against her pickup. His color was better than the day before. He was better dressed, too. This time, Ryder McKay wore a dark gray suit with a dark blue shirt and dress shoes instead of the combat boots.

His hair had a little wave to it so it managed to look tussled even short-cut. He wasn't the best looking man on his team, although he was plenty hot, but he had the kind of energy, a presence that drew her as the others hadn't. All the more annoying since she hated him for taking Esperanza away.

He was the last person she wanted to see today.

He limped toward her. Looked as if he'd been waiting for her and his presence here wasn't just an unhappy accident. Great.

"You should be resting that leg."

"Let's sit in your truck for a second."

As he looked her over, she suddenly wished that she'd bothered to slap on some makeup that morning, or that the jeans she wore didn't have a hole above her left knee.

"What happened to Esperanza?"

"She's on her way back home. Why don't we see if we can come to some agreement about how to help her?" His desert-honey gaze held hers.

Awareness zinged up her spine. She went around him and yanked the driver's-side door open.

"You should keep that locked."

"You should mind your own business." She wasn't used to having to lock anything around here.

He got in next to her, taking up way too much space. "These are different times."

So maybe they were. Smugglers. People getting shot. People disappearing. Things like that didn't normally happen in Hullett. Even if she no longer lived around here, she hated the idea of the place changing for the worse. Dylan's sister, Molly, was usually the one who hated change and wanted everything to stay the same, but for once, Grace agreed with that sentiment wholeheartedly.

She tried to take shallower breaths as Ryder's faint masculine scent, soap and aftershave filled the cab and tickled something behind her breastbone. He smelled as good as he looked. His eyes never left her face.

She reached for the cooler behind her seat and grabbed two bottles of strawberry iced tea. Homemade, her mother's recipe. Rose Cordero had been gone close to fifteen years now, taken by breast cancer. Grace's father had been trampled to death by a bull at the rodeo the same year.

She closed her eyes for a second to shut away those memories, then said, "How about a cold drink?"

He smiled at her, and she just barely held back a groan. Was that a dimple in his cheek? The way those amazingly sexy masculine lips stretched over all those white teeth…

Holy Jehoshaphat. And he hadn't even meant to dazzle her. If he ever tried to seduce a woman in earnest… She put that thought out of her head. She didn't need to think about Ryder McKay and seduction. She had things to accomplish.

"Thanks," he said, accepting the bottle. "How well do you know the local sheriff?"

"Went to high school with him and his wife. All three of us were in the same class."

He frowned, as if that annoyed him. Go figure.

"You wouldn't be investigating Esperanza's family on your own after I told you that you can't be involved in this, would you?" He raised an eyebrow as he lifted the bottle to those distracting lips.

"I promised her I'd help."

"Why is this so important to you? You have kids back in the city?"

She nearly laughed at that. "I'm hardly mother material." Some days she was fine, but at other times the past hit her so hard she could barely see straight.

"Don't you have anyone special to go back to? A husband?"

"I don't believe in marriage."

The appalled look that flashed across his face was pretty comical. Wasn't it supposed to be the other way around, men running from commitment and women starry-eyed looking for it? Not her. Her parents' marriage had been hell. Her father had loved the rodeo ten times as much as he'd ever loved her mother. Tommy's wife had divorced him when he'd gotten sick and she'd realized that the good times were over.

"What I've seen of marriages around me so far, I'd just as soon avoid." Grace drew a long swallow of cold tea. Even if she could ever trust another person enough to give her heart, she would never want to saddle someone she cared about with the mess she was these days.

"You should go home, anyway. You must have a job to get back to," Ryder was saying.

She didn't like the way he managed to attract and irritate her at the same time. She wasn't sure which she resented more. "How about I worry about my own schedule?"

"You don't want to get mixed up with the criminal element."

The muscles in her jaw tightened. "Wanting to find her family doesn't make Esperanza a criminal."

"I was talking about the people who might have made her family disappear. So what did you find out in there?" He jerked his head toward the station.

"Not a thing." Frustration coursed through her. Nothing had popped in the computer files.

"Would help if we had a picture." He took a long drink, but kept his gaze on her.

She considered that for a moment, then pulled the photo from her pocket and set it on the dashboard in front of him.

He didn't seem overly surprised that she had the picture. Maybe he'd seen Esperanza pass it over. He took the small slip of paper and looked at it, then put the photo into his pocket. "What would it take to convince you to leave town?"

"I'm not going anywhere." She had her textbooks and she had weeks before her exams. She had some time to look into all this.

He flashed her a fierce glare. "Go home."

It took work, but she gave him her sweetest smile. "I think you're confusing me with someone who's easily intimidated."

He shook his head, and from the way his forehead drew together in a frown, she got the idea that he didn't like what he was thinking. "I don't suppose you went to school with the sheriff over at Pebble Creek, too."

"I was just talking to Kenny last week. He went to school with my brother."

"Of course he did." He scratched his elbow. "Maybe I could use you as a temporary consultant. You do know your land, and the local people," he said with a good dose of reluctance after a few seconds.

Relief flooded her. She'd been prepared to go it alone, but the search would be easier with some help. "So we're going to see Kenny?"

His phone rang.

He flicked it open and listened. "Okay." He hung up, a tight look on his face. "I have some things to look into right now, but I'll be at your place to pick you up first thing in the morning. In the meanwhile, stick to the house. My team will be looking around near the border to see if we can find where Esperanza had been brought over."

"Did that call have anything to do with her?"

He flashed her an unfathomable look, opened the door and unfolded his long legs to the ground, but then turned around to hand her a card with his name and number. "If you hear shots, you call me. If anyone knocks on your door in the middle of the night, you call me. If you hear any suspicious noises around the house…"

"I call you," she finished for him. And then tried hard not to stare at the way his pants stretched across his fine behind as he strode away, favoring his bad leg.

No doubt about it, Ryder McKay was seven kinds of trouble. She thought of her small, safe, lonely apartment in Bryan—the perfect place for her at this stage of her life. Which was why she was going to do whatever she could here to help Esperanza but, after that, she definitely wasn't going to stay.

"Stick to the house," he called from his car before getting in.

"I'm thinking of a place where you could stick your orders, but since I've been raised a Texas belle, I'm not going to say it," she called back.

Chapter Four

She drove to the shopping center and picked up a few days' worth of groceries, but didn't fill up the whole pantry. She wouldn't be around that long. Esperanza's husband and children, Miguel and Rosita, would be found.

That Ryder had the gall to tell her to stay off her own land... *Not likely.* She needed to see what was going on, where people were coming over, how big a problem she had.

She needed a good horse. Time to go for a nice long ride and rediscover her land a little.

As if conjured by wishes, a beat-up horse trailer waited in her driveway when she got home, hitched to a pickup that looked as if it was held together by nothing but prayer. Old Man Murray leaned against the trailer on the shady side.

He took off his stained working hat as she got out of her truck.

"I heard you were home, Gracie. I'm awful sorry about Tommy. You let me know if there's anythin' I can do."

In his mid-nineties, the man held down a ranch that had been in his family for two centuries, abandoned by his kids who'd moved to the North-East. But he would never walk by you without asking what he could do to help.

"I'm good for now. Thanks for offering. Everything okay with you?" She nodded toward the trailer.

A troubled shadow crossed his weather-lined face. "It's Cookie. Colic, I think. I was hopin' you could check her out." He looked at his worn boots, hat in hand, as if embarrassed to be asking.

"I'm not a vet yet."

"I don't have money for the vet just now, Gracie," he admitted with a sideway glance. "I've been walkin' her and doin' the wait-and-see thing. I gotta go into the hospital tomorrow. Be there for at least a week."

Concern leaped. "Are you all right?"

"Doc Hanley says my ticker's wearin' out. Told him I don't care, but you know how damn pushy the man is. Henry will be takin' care of the animals, but the boy will have his hands full without this. His bad hip is actin' up, anyway.…"

The "boy" had been Murray's foreman at one time, stayed on after the money ran out and the rest of the ranch hands left for greener pastures. He was past seventy. And although they'd started out as employer and employee, the two men had been best friends for decades, looking out for each other.

"All right," Grace capitulated. "Let's see about this."

She opened the trailer and backed the horse out. The mare did look bloated. She pressed her ear against the horse's side. "Sounds like she swallowed a Harley."

Murray nodded. "Plenty of rumbling."

"Any pawing or lying down?"

"No. I've been watching her."

"Runny stool?"

"Loose but not runny."

She walked the horse around a little, watching carefully. The mare didn't seem to be in pain. She needed some regular hand walking in the next couple of days to work the gas out, and some medicine to calm her intestinal tract. Chamomile and belladonna would accomplish that. Colocynth and nux vom would help with the gas. She preferred homeopathic cures and focused on those in her studies. She knew a place in Hullett where she could pick up everything she needed.

She glanced toward the barn her grandfather had built not long before his death, after the old one was lost to brush fire that spared the house, thank God. A single stall could be easily cleaned.

"I have no hay, or feed," she said more to herself than to Murray.

"Brought some along, just in case."

As she looked behind the trailer, she could see that the back of the pickup was loaded.

"Okay."

"I can pay you in a couple of weeks," the old man said in a tone of pure relief.

"How about a trade? I've been missing riding. Maybe I could borrow one of your other horses for a week. That way this one wouldn't be so lonely here."

His leathery face brightened. "I'll bring you Maureen and some more feed."

"How about I'll make Cookie comfortable here, then I'll go with you." She wouldn't mind a quick look at his other animals, and a chance to tell Henry that she was here if he needed anything.

Not that she was settling in at the ranch, or regrowing roots or any of that. But while she *was* here, she could certainly help out some old friends. Temporarily.

"Don't suppose you need a barn cat?" she asked, leading the mare to the old corral that was still in pretty good shape.

"Got six kittens I don't know what to do with. Haven't seen the mother in days. Can't catch them up in the hayloft. Can barely climb the ladder to leave them food."

The idea of Murray climbing the ladder to the hayloft was enough to give her a heart attack. "A coyote probably caught the mother." She bit her lip. Oh, what the hell. "I can catch those kittens and bring them back here, if you want," she offered before common sense could take hold of her.

She had no idea what she was going to do with those kittens when she went back home to Bryan, an issue she should have been thinking about during the short ride to Murray's place. Instead, she thought of Ryder McKay.

"NOTICED YOU DIDN'T HAVE one of these," Ryder said as Grace opened the door the next morning. He held up clear plastic packaging that had a dead bolt inside. "A small thank-you gift for saving me the other night."

She was still waiting for the coffee to kick in. Her muscles ached in places that hadn't ached in a long time. She'd ridden out on Maureen after dinner, enjoyed it so much that she'd overdone it. Damn fine horse. Made her miss her old riding days. She hadn't had a horse in…forever.

Ryder was checking her windows. "If you need a security upgrade, I'm an expert in that area. I could look this place over, make a few improvements."

"It's my place. I can do whatever needs to be done to it."

"Just a friendly offer."

"We're not friends. We're going to find Paco, Miguel and Rosita, then never see each other again. We're not going to get close to each other in any way, shape or form."

"Keep our distance."

"Exactly."

"Big words from a woman who cut off my pants the first time we met," he reminded her, humor glinting in his eyes.

She turned on her heels and marched to the kitchen. She definitely needed more coffee.

She should have slept like a log after all the exercise, but she had a rough night. The ancient air-conditioning unit in the bedroom no longer worked, so she'd slept with the window open. Could hear the horses stomp around in the barn, getting used to their new surroundings. They kept waking her up, and each time it took her forever to settle back to sleep.

Ryder followed her and leaned against the counter. He wore another fancy suit. Maybe he only wore his black cargo pants and combat boots for in-the-field investigating.

He set the padlock on the counter.

"Thank you," she said, even as part of her bristled. Didn't he think that she was capable of picking up a lock for herself? The fact that he'd been thinking about her, about her safety, and cared enough to go out of his way to pick the lock up, made her feel strange. And she was feeling out of sorts already, not having gotten nearly enough sleep.

She'd spent half the night awake because of the horses, the other half tossing and turning in between nightmares that had taken her back to the battlefield.

"Did everything work out yesterday? You had to run off because of that phone call." She tried to fish for some information. She'd gotten used to teamwork in the army. It annoyed her that Ryder was obviously keeping secrets. Whatever was happening on her land, she was smack-dab in the middle of it, and had a right to know, dammit.

He watched her for a second, then seemed to come to some sort of decision. "My team found some suspicious car tracks."

"On Cordero land?"

He nodded, and her heart sank. She hadn't seen anything when she'd ridden out on Maureen. Of course, the ranch was way too big to ride every corner of it in one evening. "There's some kind of a corporate team building thing going on. Could be them." She should have probably told him that before, but he had a way of distracting her from thinking straight.

"I'll look into that. You have a number to call?"

She gave him Dylan's, and he saved it in his phone.

"Any other people come here on a regular basis?"

She shook her head. "It's not a working ranch. Hasn't been in years. The soil was never the best. My grandfather experimented with corn, milo and okra leaf cotton, and some other things. He made a good go of it most of the time. The years it failed, he had a couple hundred head of cattle to fall back on, and his horses."

"Sounds like he knew something about diversifying."

"He knew something about everything."

One of the kittens meowed and drew his attention to

the box next to the sofa. He stepped over to check out the kittens and raised an eyebrow..

"Came in last night. They lost their mother."

"Do you need to stay home to take care of them?"

"Fed them after I fed the horses this morning." She'd already walked Cookie, too. Wanted to do that a couple of times today, in between whatever else she would be doing. She already had the horse's medicine.

"Horses?"

"Long story."

Twinky strolled in, just in case he'd forgotten about her.

"That's a lot of animals you collected in three days."

She pulled her spine straight and looked him straight in the eye. "I'm just good-hearted that way." Okay, so maybe her tone was a touch too defensive.

She hated that she was so bristly these days. Couldn't take criticism. Growled at the slightest offer of help. Suddenly those things seemed to imply weakness. And she was way too self-conscious of all her new weaknesses already. She was no longer the tough soldier she'd once been. She had a hard time dealing with that. Hated every reminder. Jumped on every perceived offense.

She made a point to relax and lower her shoulders.

"I'm thinking animal hoarder." A grin played above his lips.

There. He'd been joking.

"You do have a good heart." He bent to play with the kittens.

For a big, tough soldier, he sure could be gentle when he wanted to be. The careful way he played with those kittens softened something inside her, opened her up a little.

"I used to drag home every living thing when I was younger. Gramps drew the line at skunks." She'd even brought two stray dogs onto the army base in Iraq where she had served. They were coming to the U.S. soon with her returning unit. She hoped she could work out a way to have them with her someday.

"Are you telling me this is an improvement?" he asked as he stood.

She thought about the dozen armadillos she'd liberated from the armadillo races the summer after her senior year. The old sheriff had threatened to put her in jail. Probably would have carried her off if Gramps and Tommy hadn't defended her. That had been some night. A quick smile stretched her lips. "An improvement by leaps and bounds, believe me."

A picture of those armadillos getting into the kitchen cabinets flashed into her mind, and she suddenly lost it, laughing, swallowing coffee the wrong way.

He was staring at her with a strange expression. Probably thought she was a lunatic. She did her best to pull her features back into a straight face and stop coughing.

"You don't laugh enough," he said, then blinked, as if shaking off whatever thoughts had taken hold of him. "I can put the lock up for you."

That ended all the fuzzy, relaxed feelings. She snorted. "I think I can handle a screwdriver all by my dainty little self." There she went with the overdefensiveness again, but she couldn't help it.

His upper lip twitched.

Looking at his lips made heat spread through her

belly for some reason. They seemed way too close suddenly. When had he come around the counter? Or had she? They stood at the end of the kitchen island. Looked as if they'd both come halfway.

She licked her lips nervously.

His gaze darkened.

She jumped back. Suddenly she didn't seem to be able to look him in the eye. Her gaze fell on his fancy suit.

"If we're going to be walking around town together... You can't dress like that."

He quirked an eyebrow.

"It screams outsider from a mile. People don't like strangers so much in these little towns around here. You need a pair of worn jeans and a shirt that's more appropriate."

"There's an appropriate shirt?"

"Where are you from, anyway?"

"Up north," he said vaguely.

City slicker. "You look it." She closed her eyes for a second. Made up her mind. She had to let go. "I have a couple of my brother's things in one of the upstairs closets."

"I'm not that much into overalls."

"I was thinking a couple of decent shirts." And boots.

She looked at the boot rack by the door, and he followed her gaze, let out a whistle. He was staring at a pair of silver rattlesnake skin beauties with spurs. Tommy's favorite. She'd meant to keep those.

But she drew her lungs full and gave a slow nod. "Go ahead." And went upstairs to get those shirts. Even found a pair of jeans that might be long enough for Ryder.

She happened to catch a glimpse of the barn from the upstairs window as she passed it on her way back down. The door stood wide-open. She could have sworn she'd closed it earlier. Then again, the latch was old and pretty loose. She made a mental note to take care of that before they left. It wouldn't hurt to check in on the colicky horse one more time, anyway.

By the time Ryder came out of the laundry room, all changed, she was sipping from a country blue mug, sitting in the ancient rocking chair by the window. She took one look at him then coughed as she choked on her coffee again. "You can take those spurs off. Unless you're planning on breaking in wild horses today."

The grin she struggled with said she'd pay good money to see that. But the expression on her face slowly changed to something other than mirth as he turned around to show it all off. "Do I blend in better?"

She pushed to her feet. "You'll do." And went out to the kitchen.

He swaggered after her, sat by the table and took the spurs off with a hint of regret. His great-great-grandfather, the one he'd been named after, had been a famous Oregon lawman back in the day. He imagined the man might have worn spurs like this.

She put her mug in the sink and glanced through the window. "You drive an SUV." Her tone was less than complimentary.

"I sure do." He loved that ride. It had a reinforced frame, secret compartments, special headlights, the works.

"Real men drive trucks," she muttered.

"Do they now? Are you dissing my ride?" What got

her hackles up now? She definitely had a prickly side. He found that it intrigued him.

"SUVs are just a step above soccer mom vans."

"Live with it." He raised an eyebrow, daring her to challenge him. He stepped closer, suddenly itching to show her what real men did.

But she backed down. "Could be worse, I suppose. You could be driving a hybrid."

"I happen to own a hybrid."

She watched him for a long moment, then suddenly gave a lopsided smile that drew his attention to her lips. "You do?"

He named the year, model and make—somewhat slowly. He was a little distracted.

"Actually, that's pretty nice. I'd love to have one of those someday," she admitted, rinsing her cup and heading for the door.

"Any new adventures last night?" he asked. "Any midnight visitors?"

"All quiet on the southern front. So what's the plan for today?" She strode to the barn, and he followed, appreciating her long-legged stride all the way. He'd always been partial to petite blondes, but Grace Cordero was difficult not to appreciate.

He gave her a list of the surrounding small towns he planned on visiting—bars, bus stations, boarding-houses.

"We don't have to go into Esperanza's story with everyone. I don't want to tip off the bad guys that she'd been talking to the authorities."

The barn looked abandoned, save for two stalls that had been recently cleaned. Spiderwebs and shadows in the back, piles of heaven knew what old tools and miscellaneous ranch equipment. She checked on the horses, even talked to them, admonishing them to good behavior.

"What do I say about why I'm looking for Paco?" she asked as she closed the barn door behind them on their way out.

"Stick with the friend of a friend story."

"Who do I say you are?"

"Border protection consultant surveying the area to make budget recommendations. You could also say that you're showing me around town because I'm an old friend. We could know each other from the army, or college or something. I need an introduction to people around here that'll make them trust me."

"Aren't I lucky to have so many friends," she muttered. "I came here to spread my brother's ashes."

That explained the urn on the mantel, and her eyes that could turn from flashing with indignation to haunted in a quick second. "Your visit can have multiple purposes."

"I'm not a great fan of lying."

"I can get better cooperation from people if they don't view me as a complete outsider. I think there are a number of illegal activities taking place on your land."

Her expression turned somber as she nodded.

"Which is why you need to stay in town, at a hotel, for the time being." Maybe this time she'd listen.

There flashed the indignation. "I'm not going to be run off my own land. And people would think it weird if I was around, but not staying at the house."

She had a point there. He drew a slow breath as the car flew down the highway. "If you want to stay, I should stay there with you."

Her eyes widened for a second, but she gathered herself quickly. "No way."

"It'd be safer."

"If there are smugglers out there in some remote corner of the ranch, they have no reason to tangle with me. And if they do...I'm a trained soldier."

The hard set of her jaw said there was no changing her mind about that. He was going to try, anyway. But they had other things to take care of first.

They drove on, sharing theories about where Paco and the kids might have disappeared to. They reached Pebble Creek in a little over an hour, and lucked out with Kenny. The Pebble Creek sheriff was bald and pockmarked, wearing the fanciest boots Ryder had ever seen, with swirling stitches and various color patches of leather. He came up to Ryder's shoulder, and put on an oversize Stetson in a hurry that went a long way toward negating the difference in height between them.

Grace greeted him like a friend, introduced Ryder and pulled the photo to ask about the Molineros.

The man pulled a sheet of paper from the stack on his desk. Do You Know This Man? stood in large letters on the top of the page. On the bottom was the sheriff department's insignia with a phone number to call. A police sketch of Paco took up the middle.

Grace tensed. "What did he do?"

"Showed up dead in a ditch. No ID. Nobody called the hotline, either."

"How about his kids?"

The sheriff swore under his breath as he took the picture from her. "I'm going to need a copy of this. We'll start looking immediately."

"I appreciate it." Grace's gaze strayed back to the poster. "How did he die?"

"Shot to the back of the head."

"Any leads?"

Ryder let her ask the questions. Answers tended to come faster this way.

"None. Couldn't even find the bullet. It went straight through. He'd been killed someplace else then dropped off where we found him."

"What happened to the body?" she demanded.

Kenny shrugged. "Since nobody showed up to claim it, the county buried him last week. That's a headache and a half these days. With the economy as it is, unclaimed bodies are up by a third. The county crematorium stopped accepting four months ago. The coroner had to make a deal with a private place."

He made a face. "Wanted to keep him a while longer, since he was a murder victim, but the morgue is backed up, too. They needed the space. The coroner did a thorough autopsy, but then we had to let him go. Didn't think anyone would come looking for him at this stage. Sorry, honey."

"I'll let his wife know." Her face turned grim, her eyes haunted. "Did he have any personal effects that might be returned to her?"

Kenny thought for a minute. "I'll check to be sure, but as far as I can remember, he didn't have a damn thing on him, except this." He reached over to his desk and shuffled around, picked up a Chevy emblem and handed it to her. "Could barely pry it out of his hands. No other usable prints on it, but his. I've been keeping it out as a reminder. I don't like unsolved cases."

She turned the piece of chrome over in her hand, then

handed it to Ryder. "Looks like it's from a cowboy Cadillac. It's a little larger than the ones used on sedans."

When Ryder shot her a questioning look, she said, "A pickup truck."

"Doesn't exactly narrow things down," the sheriff put in. "Must be a million pickups in the county, Chevy, Ford and Dodge for the most. Folks in these parts believe in buying American."

Ryder checked the emblem over then handed it back to the man.

"Please let me know if you find out anything about those kids," she asked the sheriff. "I'd really appreciate it."

"Anything for Tommy's little sis." He gave a sad smile. "How are you dealing with that?"

"I'm dealing all right, Kenny."

But Ryder heard a small hitch in her voice, which made him wonder just how well she was handling everything, if it hadn't been a mistake to let her put herself in the middle of all this.

Chapter Five

She spent another restless night, thinking about Miguel and Rosita, thinking who else she could have talked to over in Pebble Creek, where she'd spent most of the previous day with Ryder. She'd taken him to all her old hangouts, shown the photo to every friend she had there. Nobody remembered seeing Paco or the kids.

Grace yawned, padding down the stairs as the sun rose outside. The horses were less anxious their second night than the first, but some noise in the barn had still woken her up at dawn, and she hadn't been able to fall back asleep. Might as well get started on her day.

Ryder had said he'd be coming by first thing in the morning. Hopefully not too early. A nice, peaceful hour or so—just her and her coffee mug—would be great.

She headed straight for the coffeemaker. She was on her second cup when a pickup pulled into her driveway. She looked out the window, then went to the door to unlock it, still thinking of Ryder as she turned the dead bolt.

"Hello, Dylan." She glanced at his new pickup in the driveway, a Chevy, the emblem in place. She couldn't believe she checked. This whole mess was starting to make her paranoid.

"Sorry to come so early. I had to run some errands this morning, but I wanted to check on you before I got going." He looked drawn, as if he hadn't been getting enough sleep, either. He looked her over. "How are you this morning?"

"Sleepy." She motioned him in. "Coffee?"

"That'd be much appreciated."

"Dylan," she said as they headed into the kitchen, "Have you heard anything about smuggling going on around here? Have you ever seen anything?"

He stopped to look at her, his eyes narrowing. "Did something happen?"

She hesitated. Ryder had said not to tell anyone that he'd been shot on her land.

"I drove out a little yesterday. I thought I saw some tracks." Great. Now she was lying to Dylan.

He tensed. "Could be someone looking for their lost cattle or whatever. Or rustlers. With the economy the way it is, rustling is becoming big business again. It's like the Wild West days are coming back."

"Oh, God, remember Gramps's rustling stories?" She smiled as she strode to the counter and poured him a mug of steaming java.

"He told the best stories, hands down." Dylan smiled, too, and took the coffee. "Thanks."

"How long is the team-building group staying?"

"They're leaving this morning. Another group is coming in two weeks. They're way down by the ravine. They won't be in your way."

But they could be in Ryder's. She took a sip of her coffee, and decided she would let Ryder deal with that.

"On the off chance that the tracks you saw do belong to rustlers... You should stay with Molly," Dylan said, but before she could think of a way to say no without making it seem as if she didn't want to spend time with her old friend, another car pulled up her driveway.

She opened the door.

"Ready?" Ryder looked all freshly scrubbed, smelling of soap and aftershave. The sun was behind him, outlining his wide shoulders. When he smiled at her and that dimple appeared, her heart rate picked up a little.

Then his smile dimmed when Dylan walked out of the kitchen.

"Ryder McKay, Dylan Rogers." She performed the introductions and kissed goodbye her dreams of a solitary, peaceful morning that would let her come gradually awake at her own pace.

"Dylan is an old friend of mine," she told Ryder, who was busy measuring the man up. "Ryder is a friend from the army. Works for CBP now." Yet another lie. She didn't like the way things were going in her life lately, yet she didn't see a way out, either. Something she needed to think about.

Dylan stiffened. "He's wearing Tommy's boots."

The two looked at each other like two seasoned gunslingers, ready to issue an invitation to meet at high noon in the street in front of the saloon. *Wild West, indeed.*

Dylan hooked his thumbs into his belt loops and puffed out his chest an inch. Unlike Ryder, he didn't need tutoring on how to look every inch the cowboy. Yet, even if Ryder didn't wear the clothes as naturally as Dylan, he sure looked good in them. Dylan no longer worked the fields, and had lost that leanness that came with daily physical labor.

Ryder had all kinds of physical strength in spades.

He was a warrior through and through, and there was no mistaking it.

She caught herself comparing the two and stopped it. She didn't need to give that much thought to either man. She had more important things on her agenda than deciding which one looked better in blue jeans. *Ryder.*

"So you're the border agent?" Dylan asked him, and managed to make the question sound like an insult. A lot of people in these parts had definite opinions on the ineffectiveness of border protection.

Ryder nodded. "We talked on the phone. I appreciate your cooperation. I haven't received those schedules yet for the leadership training groups you have out there, though."

"Secretary must have forgotten to email it," Dylan said in an impassive tone.

"How about coffee?" she offered Ryder to ease the tension.

Once she herded them into the kitchen, Dylan got a cup from the cupboard, as if to show off that he knew where everything was, that he belonged here, with her. She definitely sensed some territorial, alpha male sort of posturing between the two, which bewildered her more than a little.

It wasn't as if either man was interested in her. Probably just some automatic testosterone response. Dylan was used to being top cowboy, and Ryder was probably used to being top gun. They were both born to dominate their environment.

"I have some business to take care of in Edinburg today," Dylan told her as he held out the empty cup for her to fill. "But I'll come back tonight. I'll stay with you while you're here. No sense taking any chances."

He set the cup in front of Ryder with a hard click on the counter.

"No need for you to worry about that. My team and I will make sure she's okay," Ryder said cheerfully, looking oh so innocent, but obviously egging the man on.

"I'll be fine," she told them both. "I have Gramps's rifle."

"And I brought her a good lock for the door," Ryder put in.

Dylan looked between them. He seemed to be struggling with something for a few seconds, but then he finished his coffee and headed for the door with undisguised reluctance. "I'd better get on the road if I'm going to make that appointment. If you need anything, Grace, just call me."

She walked him out. "Thanks for stopping in and checking on me, but I'm fine here. Really."

He watched her without saying a word.

"Ryder is a friend. I knew him in the army." Best to stick with that story.

He waited another moment, then hugged her before he strode away.

When she walked back to the kitchen, Ryder had a map spread on the counter, with her land, smack-dab in the middle, outlined in black marker.

He drew his index finger along the line that indicated the border, erratically drawn by the Rio Grande. Then he tapped his finger on the southernmost corner of her land. "Rough terrain."

"There are a few old dirt roads that might be still passable." She pointed them out.

Since they were looking at the map together, they were standing close enough for his scent to invade her senses. His body had this energy field that drew her. The closer she got, the stronger the draw became. Her skin tingled, honest to God, which was so wrong.

Her body was developing some sort of a crush on him. Luckily, her mind was strong enough to reject the whole nonsense. She wasn't having any of it. She stepped back.

"Is Dylan renting the whole ranch?" He looked up from the map and held her gaze.

She nodded. "But he only uses the area around the ravine for the team building camps. They want a sense of isolation. So please don't go barging into their camp. I don't want you to mess up Dylan's business."

He flashed her a curious look. "There was nobody out there when I checked the place last week."

"Maybe they came after you checked. Or you looked in the wrong area. It's a big ranch. There are a lot of rocky parts other than the ravine."

He folded the map and tucked it away, his gaze fast on her face. "So what kept you up last night?"

She flinched and looked away. The dark circles under her eyes were probably hard to miss. "Every little noise wakes me up. I keep thinking... You were shot on my ranch. Do you think Paco was killed here?"

The possibility had occurred to her at one point, and she had a hard time letting go of it.

"Nothing points to that. He came through the border with a visa, legally. I was shot by smugglers. If there's a connection, so far I'm not seeing it."

She nodded.

"But just because I don't think Paco was shot on your land, it doesn't mean I think you're safe. *I* was shot here."

Right. She couldn't argue with that.

"Either you go to a hotel, or I'll be staying here with you."

She didn't do well with ultimatums. "Or how about we play that I'm boss on my own ranch, and I decide what happens?" she snapped. Her nerves might have been a little jumpy these days, but that didn't mean that either Dylan or Ryder had to babysit her.

She could defend herself if worse came to worst. She'd shot men before; she could shoot another. Except, she really didn't want to have to. She found reentering civilian life difficult enough already. She wanted peace and normalcy.

Trouble was coming. She felt it in her bones. The idea of walking away from it was tempting, and not just to the nearest hotel, but all the way back to her apartment in Bryan. Yet Ryder's top priority was to find the smugglers and stop the trafficking across the border. He could get distracted from finding Miguel and Rosita. They needed to be someone's first priority.

Kenny was looking for them, but he had a whole police department to run, and they weren't even sure if the kids had disappeared in Pebble Creek. The father's body had been dumped there, but he hadn't been killed where they'd found him.

Those kids needed an advocate, someone to push for them, someone to make sure they weren't forgotten, didn't simply become a statistic. She looked at Ryder and silently swore that with or without him, she was going to find Rosita and Miguel.

"I'm staying here. Nobody is staying with me. End of story," she told him.

THEY WENT TO PEBBLE CREEK first, then Hullett—where Ryder and Grace had spent hours talking to business owners in vain. They all insisted that they'd never seen Paco Molinero. They also all denied hiring illegals or knowing anything about smuggling in the area. Even Grace's connections didn't help. As Ryder drove her back home, he was humming with frustration.

He'd been in a bad mood to start with. Ever since he'd bumped into that Dylan guy at her house this morning, in fact. He'd run the man through the system after Grace had given him Dylan's name and number. Everyone who spent time on her land was a suspect.

The corporate team-building training could have been a cover. Except it wasn't. Everything checked out. Every sign pointed toward Dylan Rogers being a legitimate businessman, well loved by people in town who still remembered his high school glory days.

And a close friend of Grace from the looks of it. For some reason, the thought made his jaw muscles tighten.

"So what's next for you?" she wanted to know.

"Drive around, see if I can find some tracks. Maybe I'll stumble on the crossing point by accident. About the only chance we have of finding it in an area this large." The fact that they couldn't call on local law to help slowed them at every step.

He was used to fighting foreign enemies, was used to treachery and all sorts of depravity, of having his guard up at all times. That he still had to be on guard, here in the U.S., bugged him. His mission would have been a hundred times easier if he didn't have to worry about crooked border agents or crooked cops.

Sure, ninety-nine percent of them were fine, the best of the best, but because of the one percent who had mixed loyalties, he couldn't trust any of them. He didn't understand that—people messing with their own country. The country too many of his good friends had died protecting.

"I'll go with you," she offered.

He hesitated—not because he didn't trust her. He was good at reading people, and she was as straight an arrow as there ever was. But he wasn't entirely crazy about the idea of her getting more involved. He didn't want harm to come to her. Sentimental nonsense for a soldier. One of his team's goals was to develop local assets. She was one. Nothing about this was personal.

Yet he found himself thinking about her in the night, worrying about her. Part of him wanted to pack her up and ship her out. Another part of him wanted to tell her more about the operation and ask her opinion. She was pretty sharp. She was a local. She might come up with an insight that had escaped his team.

"So you pretty much know every inch of this land?"

"Grew up on it. We used to ride all over, hunt, camp, herd cattle on the northeast pastures where the soil is decent enough to support grass."

He looked over the inhospitable terrain they were crossing at the moment, nothing but clumps of scraggly weeds, patches of dry brush here and there, and some mesquite. The landscape did hold some stark beauty, even if it was alien to him—prickly and unwelcoming.

"All right. If you have nothing else to do. Okay." He

drove her home, and she checked on the kittens, then on the horses.

The one called Cookie seemed to be doing better. She walked the mare for twenty minutes or so, Ryder beside her, asking her about growing up on the borderlands. She was easy to talk to. When she had a mind to cooperate. Funny, too. He almost envied her childhood by the end, growing up around animals, on all this open land. Sounded very different from his childhood in a town house in Seattle.

"The best way to find out what's going on out there is on horseback," she said as she tied Cookie back in her stall. "You miss too much in a truck, no matter how slow you're going. Do you ride?"

"A little." He'd had to learn on an op, and in a hurry.

"Too bad Cookie isn't up to riding yet." She looked at the horse wistfully.

"How about the other one?"

She patted the massive black mare that stood tall and proud next to her. "Maureen is a dream."

"We could ride double."

She looked him over. Hesitated.

"Or I could go alone."

"We'll ride double," she said immediately, and he bit back a smile. "If Maureen is okay with it. We'll have to see. I do have a bigger saddle around here somewhere."

She found it after a brief search and began saddling up the horse. He helped by handing her whatever she needed next.

"I think Esperanza came over in a tunnel." His instincts said he could trust her with that piece of information. The line of work he was in frequently required life-and-death decisions to be made in an instant, on nothing but instinct. He'd learned to trust his. "Any idea where the entrance to something like that might be on your land?"

"A tunnel under the river?"

"It's not impossible."

She shot him a look of denial, but then gave the question some thought before she responded. "*If* there's something like that, it would be close to the border. They wouldn't want to dig more than necessary."

He'd looked, along with his team, but they hadn't found anything. "The tunnel's entrance would be covered up, most likely." But someone who knew the land intimately might be able to pick out what looked out of place. And being on horseback would probably help, too. She was right about that.

When she was done with the horse, he led the animal out of the barn and boosted her up. For once, she didn't protest the help.

"Get up behind me," she said, scooting forward as far as she could, holding the reins.

Because, of course, she was driving.

He bit back another grin. An animal hoarder with control issues. Sounded like a mess, but she wasn't. She got done everything that needed to get done and then some. Never backed down when it came to saving anything, either, be it animals or people.

She kept her left foot out of the stirrup, so he could use it for leverage. She gave him a hand. Then he was up behind her, her lean body between his thighs. The heat that shot through him caught him off guard. And that was before he put his arm around her to hang on to the saddle horn in front of her.

She put both feet in the stirrups and clicked her

tongue, started Maureen in an easy walk, just a small circle. "She seems to be handling it well. Some horses buck when they're ridden double." After another minute, she directed the horse toward the fields.

"I don't want to push her too hard. There's a place I'm thinking of. We'll ride out there, then back. I don't want to ride her too long with all this weight."

"Are you disparaging my figure?"

She gave a snort.

He could find nothing wrong with her figure, certainly. Which he'd known before, but the fact was brought to his attention anew, now that his body was practically wrapped around hers.

She followed a dirt road for a while, then turned onto what looked like an animal trail.

"Deer and wild hogs," she said.

And he was glad he had his weapon tucked behind his back.

They rode quietly for a couple of miles. When he spotted some tire tracks in the dust, he pointed them out to her.

"Probably from the team-building training."

Soon the ground turned rocky, washed out by flash floods over the last few decades from the looks of it. His SUV definitely couldn't have made it through here. "Where are we going?"

"To the border near the ravine," she told him. "It's a shortcut. The path someone on foot might use to cut through the acres as fast as possible toward reaching Hullett."

When they got to a watering hole, they let the horse drink and rest while they walked around to check for signs that anyone had been here. Grace found an empty plastic bottle in the brush.

"Could be from anyone," she said. "Hikers, border patrol, the team Dylan has out this way."

He agreed, but checked the GPS on his phone and saved the coordinates. Might be worth staking out for a couple of nights to see if the smugglers came this way. This was exactly the kind of spot they needed to be watching, but would be nearly impossible to find without the help of someone who knew the land.

They got back on the horse and rode south, taking their time, making sure they weren't pushing Maureen too hard.

An hour passed before Grace stopped the horse again, having reached a rocky area. "We'll walk from here."

Nothing but dust and rocks and cacti as far as the eye could see, prickly pear in abundance. They walked through the inhospitable landscape, leading the horse.

"Watch for snakes," she told him.

She didn't have to. He'd been watching all this time. He'd seen a couple of beauties while he and his team had been familiarizing themselves with the borderlands.

Soon they came out at the top of a long ravine, a flat area with a road leading to it from the opposite direction. Someone had parked here not long ago; he noted the tire marks. A single vehicle. Boot prints all around.

She tied the horse to a mesquite brush and pushed forward, wiping the sweat from her forehead. "This way."

She might not have trusted him or the government he worked for, but she was willing to help, willing to go the extra mile. In pretty much everything, he noted. For Esperanza and her family. For the animals that she took in.

He worked with the best of the best, men who were heroes in their own right. He wasn't easily impressed, but Grace Cordero managed to impress him.

That appreciation wouldn't have been a dangerous thing on its own, but coupled with the attraction he felt for her... He definitely needed to keep that in check. She wasn't the kind of woman he was looking for. He needed to focus on his goals and not get distracted by a woman who had fragility at her core, but at the same time acted consistently heroic.

Of course, he found that intriguing. Who wouldn't? The fact that he'd thought about kissing her didn't mean anything. She was pretty damned sexy. He couldn't imagine any red-blooded man not wanting her. A thought that suddenly made him uncomfortable.

Dylan at her house that morning... The Dylan guy was no good for her, obviously. He wouldn't have a clue what she'd gone through during her deployments. He couldn't begin to know what she needed. She needed a whole different type of man. Ryder hoped she was smart enough to know that.

"So Dylan seemed to feel very at home at your ranch," he said, not without some resentment.

She looked at him over her shoulder. "None of your business. You've invaded my land. Don't think you're going to invade my personal life, too."

He raised a hand, palm out. "Wouldn't dream of it."

But of course he did—dream of her. He dreamed of her plenty.

THE RIDE SHOOK HER UP. She liked his masculine body wrapped around hers way too much. And Grace definitely didn't want to like him that way. *Any* way. She'd be gone in a couple of days, as soon as they found Esperanza's children, and then they would never see each other again.

But, darn it, her body still tingled. What on earth was wrong with her? She didn't normally respond to strange men as strong as that.

He followed her as she started down a path nobody could have made out—unless they'd been down it a hundred times as a kid—despite her grandfather's warnings. Rocks rolled under her feet, slowing her, unbalancing her every couple of steps. No vegetation to hang on to here, nothing solid. If she grabbed on to a bigger rock, that could roll along, too, and bring her with it.

"Careful," she called behind her just as Ryder slipped.

She had one second to wish he'd worn his combat boots instead of the cowboy boots that hadn't been made for this terrain. He tried to catch himself, but the rocks gave way and he barreled toward her. He outweighed her by thirty pounds, at least. No way was she going to catch him.

Yet she had to try, because he was going to go over the edge, and his tumble would be nasty, most likely ending with a lot of broken bones.

She spread her feet and wedged in her heels, braced her body for absorbing the impact of him plowing into her.

"Out of the way!" He threw his weight to the side to avoid her, but she stood her ground and leaned into his path to catch him.

"Grace!"

For a second, his progress halted and they hung in

balance. Then the gravel under her feet gave and she slid back. She went down hard on her knees, heard her jeans rip. He tumbled with her, then caught her somehow, his arms tight around her and holding her in place just as they would have gone over the edge of the precipice.

They were on the last large rock, she on the bottom and he on top of her. A long, hard drop below them.

As he looked at her, his eyes were a soft, tawny brown, a contrast to his hard-muscled body. "Are you hurt?"

Dazed. A long time had passed since she'd last felt the weight of a man on top of her. And Ryder McKay was definitely no ordinary man. Awareness arched between them suddenly. And she found she couldn't say a word. She simply stared up at him. *My, what chiseled lips you have,* a stupid little voice said in her head.

She really shouldn't be staring at his lips. Yet she didn't seem to be able to stop. She forced her eyes shut before he could notice.

She hated the stupid attraction. Wrong man. Terrible timing.

"I'm going to get off you," he said. "Don't move. I don't want either of us going over the edge."

They were in complete agreement on that. The first thing they were in complete agreement over, in fact, since they'd met, it seemed. She opened her eyes just as his lips pulled away.

He pulled back inch by inch, moving down her body. Her shirt must have come untucked and her skin exposed, because soon she could feel his hot breath on her belly. Something twitched deep inside her. She closed her eyes and tried thinking of icebergs.

She also did her best to keep her breathing even. A

sudden adrenaline rush was the sort of thing that usually sent her emotions careening out of control, bringing back gruesome visions of battle, unbalancing her. Except, this time all she could think of was Ryder on top of her.

"Turn on your stomach and back up on all fours," he recommended when he retreated to a safe spot.

She groaned, but shifted slowly onto her stomach. Her knees burned where the gravel had scraped off the skin. Her ribs ached. She shook off the pain and focused on what she needed to do, checking for more loose rocks that could mean trouble. Her head was over the edge and she could see down; the edge of the rock hung out over some kind of a small cavern.

The entrance looked as if it might have been natural, but from her position she could see in a couple of yards, could see the four-by-fours that provided structural support a few feet in. It almost looked like the entrance to an old mine shaft, except, as far as she knew, there'd never been any mining anywhere around here.

Her stomach sank as she swore under her breath. "I think I found the tunnel."

A moment of tense silence passed.

"Don't think about that now. Just move back carefully," he said.

She did, while he did his best to guide her, then he pulled her up and held on to her maybe a little longer than was necessary.

He stepped away abruptly. "Let me see that tunnel." He went around her and eased out onto the ledge, lay on his stomach and looked down. Whistled. "Nice catch. We would have never found that. About two feet by four, has structural supports. I can only see in a few yards. Looks like it goes around the ravine."

"But how do people climb up? Women and children. In the night."

He looked for a few seconds. "They don't. They climb down. They have the plateau in front of the entrance, then if they go sideways there's a ledge at least two feet wide, wider in places. They go to the bottom of the ravine, then walk north to the end of it and walk out as the bottom slopes up."

He eased back to her, to a spot where he could safely stand, then reached up and began to unbutton his shirt, revealing a smooth expanse of muscles.

"What are you doing?" She stepped back, too quickly, stopping herself before she could tumble again.

"I'm going to save the GPS coordinates, but I want to mark the exact spot, too. I don't have anything else."

"Hold on." She wasn't sure she could handle the ride back with him half-naked on the horse behind her. "Let me."

She unbuttoned her top two buttons then yanked the shirt over her head. She had a tank top underneath.

He stared at her in a funny kind of way.

She lay the red shirt on the ground and put a large rock in the middle so the wind wouldn't blow it away. She glanced toward the edge where they'd nearly fallen to their death. "This is plain dangerous."

"Very dangerous," he murmured behind her.

Chapter Six

"The area is too big. We'd need the help, not to mention permission from the Mexican Army to search it," Ryder said into his headset, sitting behind the monitor at the office, linked to satellite maps. He noted down a half-dozen coordinates where the other end of the tunnel might be on the opposite side of the border.

Since he was good at multitasking, he also gave some thought to how good Grace had felt under him the week before on that ledge at the ravine. She had curves her no-nonsense, practical clothes did a good job of hiding, curves that made him want to embark on a more thorough discovery.

When she'd taken her shirt off... *Wowza*. His fingers had itched to grab her tank top and send it after the shirt. He wanted to see her, to touch her, her skin under his fingertips.

Not that something like that could ever happen.

He was in the market for a wife, not a rash affair. He was going to build a family.

As soon as this nasty business was over.

He didn't like the fact that he had to remind himself of those plans more and more frequently these days.

"Half of those guys are on the take from the smugglers. We can no more involve them than we can in-volve people on our side," Shep said on the other end of the line. He was in the field while Ryder was stuck behind the desk.

He took one last look on the screen at the Mexican side of the border, then scrolled the map and zoomed in on the Cordero ranch. He considered where the stra-tegic positions would have to be set up to capture the men his team hunted. Mo and Ray were out there right now, doing recon, observing, making in-field notes they could pass on to Colonel Wilson at the team's Wash-ington headquarters.

Grace had been out there again this morning. She'd volunteered to consult with them on the ranch's topog-raphy. Since she'd found the entrance, they'd had at least two men on detail at the tunnel every night, hid-den at a safe distance. At this stage, they were just ob-serving, not engaging.

They wouldn't want to tip their hand. They didn't want anyone to know that the tunnel's location had been discovered. They wanted the terrorist bastards to come through there, instead of changing plans and possibly sneaking through at another place. The bas-tards couldn't be allowed to slip through, under any circumstances.

He kept working the map. "Smugglers have a regular route right across the Cordero ranch, no doubt about it."

"We need to figure out how big the volume is. Does it go beyond human trafficking to drugs and weapons?"

"Either way, Grace is way too close to danger. She needs to leave." The tunnel had been found. She'd in-troduced him to all the key people in town and they'd accepted him as her friend, would talk to him again if he had questions. The team no longer needed her help.

"Can I go with you when you tell her that?" Shep laughed on the other end. "That shower of sparks when you two lock horns is kind of fun to watch. We don't get much entertainment out here."

He was about to put the idiot in his place when his phone rang. "Got another call."

"All right. I'll check in if we find anything."

He pushed a button, ending one call as he picked up the other.

"Everything all right down there?" Colonel Wilson didn't believe in wasting time on niceties. He was a cut-to-the-chase type of person. "Should I be sending more men?"

"I don't think that will be necessary, sir. For now, observation is all we're doing there. Sending in the cavalry at this stage would just make us all look suspicious."

"If that's your assessment of the situation, then let's go with that. Nice work on locating the tunnel, by the way. Knowing exactly where they'll be coming through will make our job a lot easier." Relief came through in the man's voice.

"Yes, sir."

"Is there anything I can help you with from here?"

He hesitated. "Can you run a high-level check on Paco Molinero?" They'd already run the basic report, and Grace had the sheriff check the local database, but since neither of those turned up anything, it couldn't hurt to go deeper. The Colonel had access to databases the average law enforcement officer didn't even know about.

The SDDU had considerable resources and very little

oversight. Few higher-up politicians even knew about the existence of the small special commando team. They worked on national security ops Stateside and abroad, and reported to Colonel Wilson, who owed explanation to no one else but the Secretary of Homeland Security.

Federal law prohibited the U.S. military from being used in the U.S. to enforce domestic law, but since the SDDU was a free-floating unit, not under the jurisdiction of any of the military branches, they had greater flexibility.

"How does Molinero figure into the op?" the Colonel wanted to know.

"I'm not sure he does, sir." He had no proof that Paco's death was related to the smugglers.

A moment of silence passed on the other end. "Is this a personal matter?"

"Yes, sir." He winced. Now was not the best time to appear anything but focused. The op his team was working on was top priority, and the Colonel was watching them to see who would be a good team leader for the new location. Ryder and Ray had been with the SDDU the longest. The Colonel would be making a choice between them, and soon, before the rest of the men arrived for the takedown.

"It's important to you?" the Colonel asked, his tone implying: *it had better not be more important than the mission.*

Ryder thought of Grace Cordero and that picture of the Molinero family she'd given him. "Yes, sir."

While they'd been busy mapping the area around the tunnel and observing the careful comings and goings of a half-dozen smugglers over the past week, she'd been busy searching for the Molinero kids with a dogged determination that had earned the respect of his team. And made him worry.

She could be walking into serious trouble if she kept pushing. And she *would* keep pushing. She wasn't the type to quit a job before it was finished.

"Is this going to be a distraction?" the Colonel was asking on the other end.

"Absolutely not, sir."

"I'll look into it."

"Thank you, sir."

His email pinged as he hung up. The border crossing logs had come in finally. About time. Over a damn week had passed since he'd requested them. He could have had them instantly, but chose to go through regular channels in the interest of keeping his cover. He wasn't ready to reveal yet that they weren't just a bunch of bureaucrats, but a superteam with superpowers.

He opened the spreadsheet and scanned through it. He found Paco Molinero's name in the logs fairly easily. There was a date for his crossing. His children's names were right next to his.

He looked for the company agent who had accompanied them. Esperanza had said his name was Dave Snebl. That name didn't pop, but the database did have a Davey Schnebly.

He scanned through the timed camera log next and froze the right frame when he got to it, then sent the man's picture to the cell phones of the others on his team. He also printed a hard copy while he ran a quick search to see how often Schnebly crossed the border. A dozen times at various border crossing points last month alone. If they could catch him… Ryder was trying to figure out how to do that when his cell phone rang again.

"They blew up the tunnel." Mo wheezed at the other end.

Ryder shot to his feet, his blood going cold, his fingers gripping the phone so tight that the plastic creaked in protest. "Who?"

"Don't know. A group came through, women and children. Their guide was robbing them. He was about to rape one of the women who didn't have any extra money to give him. It was bad, Ryder. He smacked her kid around. Ray broke cover. The bastard ran back into the tunnel before we could catch up with him. So did all the people he'd been bringing over. They took us for border patrol."

Mo grunted, as if lifting something heavy. "Ray went after them. The guide must have had the explosives set up and in place in case the tunnel was discovered. Ray hadn't come out yet." The sound of rocks rolling and clinking came through the line. He was probably digging by hand.

"Grace had gone home, right?" Ryder ran for the door, grateful that his leg was healing well. "Wasn't she supposed to go to the hospital in Hullett to see a friend?"

"She came back." Mo sounded miserable. "I don't see her."

"Find her." He leaped down the stairs and ripped the SUV's door open and jumped in. "I'm on my way. I'll bring the others."

He hung up and called the rest of the team. Shep was at the wire mill, snooping around. Jamie with his bad legs and Keith, the youngest of the team, were canvassing nearby ranches for tracks that would indicate alternate smuggling routes. Just because they'd found the tunnel didn't mean they could now grow complacent.

His car flew over the road. He cursed himself a hundred times. He should have never allowed Grace Cordero any part in this. He should have done a better job scaring her off right at the beginning. If she still resisted, he could have taken her into protective custody if needed.

He drove as fast as the car could take it, given the dirt roads. He only slowed down when he almost turned the SUV over while trying to avoid an armadillo.

By the time he reached the ravine, Ray had already dug himself out with Mo's help, but Grace was still nowhere to be found. Jamie and Keith were there already, helping Mo dig. Ray tried, but could barely stand. Looked like his leg might be broken.

"Sit down," Jamie barked at him. "You'll do more damage."

Ray shot him a dark look then tried again. "You've gotten bossier since you became an uncle, you know that? I thought it'd be a softening experience."

"Where did you see her last?" Ryder jumped into the frenetic digging, barely registering the exchange.

"Right around here, somewhere." Mo coughed from the flying dust. "As soon as we saw people coming over, we pulled into cover. But when the tunnel blew up, she rushed forward to help."

That sounded like Grace.

"Then this section caved with her right on top of it," Mo finished.

His hands never stopped moving. Neither did the other men's, not when rocks scraped their skin raw or a jagged edge drew blood. They dug like madmen, trying to get to her.

Shep arrived at last and ran to help. "How many were caught in the tunnel?"

"Half-dozen Mexicans, plus their guide and Grace."

"We have to call in outside help."

"I already did," Ray said behind him, his voice tight with tension.

They were all grim as they worked with superhuman strength, probably thinking the same thing: their carefully set up op was finished as far as secrecy went. The tunnel was lost. They would have to start everything over.

But they didn't have time to worry about any of that now.

Ryder lifted a small boulder and tossed it aside.

They'd dug down two feet in a couple of minutes. She wasn't there. He straightened for a second, mad with worry, trying to think. Rocks were strewn everywhere, the dust still settling. The explosion had shaken the ground; part of the ridge had collapsed and tumbled down into the ravine.

If Grace had been standing on the exact wrong spot... His blood ran cold. What if she wasn't under the rubble here? What if she'd tumbled over the edge?

"Get me rope." Ryder inched forward to look for a way down, careful that he didn't send more stones rolling. Couldn't see anything but dust and rocks down there. He had to try, anyway.

Shep came back a few minutes later with rope and set up a harness in seconds.

"Don't come too close to the edge," Ryder warned. "Grace!" he yelled down as he began lowering himself, Shep spotting the rope. The others kept digging at the tunnel.

"Grace!"

No response came.

She was likely covered in dust or gravel, best-case scenario. He didn't want to think about the possibility of her not getting caught on the ledge and falling all the way to the bottom of the ravine.

His heart raced as fast as his mind. He was always good at keeping his cool, but not today. "Grace!"

He coughed from the dust, but kept lowering himself, hands and feet on the rope. He didn't dare brace his feet on the unstable rock wall for fear of loosening more stones. His bullet wound pulled, but he ignored the pain.

When he reached the ledge, he tested it before letting go of the rope and putting his full weight on it. If Grace had fallen only this far, she could have made it. The drop below was not survivable.

He scanned the pile of rocks, but he didn't see her anywhere.

"Grace!" he called, inching forward carefully, searching through the rubble, his heart tightening with every passing minute.

"You see her?" came the question from above.

"Not yet." But he *would* find her, and she would be okay, because the alternative was unthinkable.

Years seemed to pass before he heard a faint cough from behind a bigger boulder. Hope leaping, he made his way over and saw her face, covered in white dust. Most of her body was buried, her head looking more like an unusual rock than anything human.

He cleared the rubble that covered her body, tossing rocks over the ledge like a madman. "Where does it hurt?"

"Everywhere." She coughed again and sat up carefully, covered in cuts and bruises, her clothes in tatters.

He squatted next to her to support her. "Did you hit your head?"

"What do you think?"

"Did you lose consciousness?"

"I wish."

Snappy to the end. Relief washed through him. He waited until she recovered a little before he helped her to stand. Sirens sounded in the distance.

She winced as she put weight on her right foot. "I don't think my ankle made it."

"Get on my back," he said, at the same time as she said, "Help me snap my ankle back in."

She had grit, and plenty of it.

She walked him through how to do it, biting her lip hard when the small pop indicated at last that he'd found the right place. His jaw drew tight. He hated that she was in pain, and he hated it even more that he'd caused some of it.

He ripped off his shirt, rolled it and wrapped it tight to stabilize the ankle, scowling at her when she hopped aside once he was done. "You still shouldn't put weight on that foot."

"I'm not planning to. Let's go up while the going is good." She reached for the rope.

"She's coming up," he called out to warn Shep to brace. And blinked hard as she started up, using nothing but her arms.

She didn't have an ounce of extra weight on her, and she was still in top military shape, obviously. But the display of strength still surprised him. It was pretty amazing.

And hot. If he wasn't so damned worried about her, he would have been awash in lust. His emotions were all over the place, and he hated the feeling, so he shook it off and tried to get back to his commando core.

He waited until she was all the way up and pulled over the edge before he put his own weight on the rope and climbed up after her.

The first of the ambulances arrived. Ray was fighting off one of the paramedics, Grace trying to escape the other.

"I'm fine. Worry about the people who are trapped in the tunnel." But, after some argument, she did let the guy remove Ryder's shirt and bind her ankle so it wouldn't pop out again when she tried to walk.

"We got an opening!" Mo shouted from a hundred yards away.

The two police officers jumping out of the first cop car on the scene ran right to him. The paramedics gave up on Ray and Grace and rushed over, too, just as a fire truck pulled in.

"I'm taking you two to the hospital," Ryder told them.

"I didn't break anything." She rushed forward to help.

"Like hell," Ray muttered through clenched teeth, balancing on one foot, holding his other leg out of the way.

He thought about knocking Ray out and stashing him in the car, then tackling Grace and taking her by force. But he didn't want to risk injuring her further. And since most of the arriving emergency personnel were greeting her by name and seemed to be friends of hers, he figured they might come to her defense if he started manhandling her.

He strode forward.

"You take that guy," he said to a burly fireman, pointing to Ray, "and get him to the E.R. to have his leg put in a cast, no matter what he says."

The man looked at the big chunk of Viking and shook his head. "Me and what army?"

"Sedate him."

"Left my big game dart gun in my other car."

Jamie was coming over. "Let me handle this."

That taken care of, Ryder ran after Grace and grabbed her by the elbow. "I want you to go with Ray and get checked out."

She gave him an impatient shove. "There's no time for that. I'm okay."

Like hell she was. But before he could argue, Mo gave a shout from the head of the line. "I got someone here."

And the rescue began in earnest.

He made sure he stuck close to Grace as people formed a chain and handed football-size stones back, clearing the hole. Once the opening was large enough, they helped people out one after the other, bleeding women and children covered in dust and scrapes.

Then they brought out a body, Caucasian male, late twenties. He had a pistol tucked behind his oversize belt buckle, and another in his cowboy boots. His face was muddy with blood and rock dust, but Ryder recognized him. "Davey Schnebly. This is the guy who brought Esperanza Molinero over."

"He won't be making any more trips," Mo said in a grim tone.

They'd wanted to find the man, but not in this kind of shape. He could have been a useful lead.

Keith searched the body, found nothing else, so they turned Schnebly over to the sheriff.

The ambulances were leaving.

Ryder left the others and strode back to where Grace was leaning against a boulder. She wiped sweat from her forehead, looking pale and shaky.

"Sit down," Ryder snapped at her. He still wasn't over the scare that she could have gotten hurt or worse.

She did as she was told, sinking to a larger rock. What? No argument?

He flashed her a narrow-eyed look. "Are you okay?"

"I'm a little dizzy. I didn't think I got hurt, but I could be wrong," she admitted. "I might have a slight concussion."

He swore under his breath. Wasn't there a saying about doctors making the worst patients? He picked her up carefully and strode away from the rest of his team, depositing her onto the front passenger seat of his SUV and ignoring the curious looks the others were giving him.

"I'm taking her to the hospital," he told them, then tore out of there as if his life depended on it.

Because Grace Cordero's did.

God knew what injuries she had sustained in that fall, then aggravated during the rescue.

Her eyes were closed, her head leaning back against the headrest. Definitely pale. He'd been so focused on her ankle, he realized suddenly, that he hadn't even considered other things. Like internal bleeding.

SHE LAY ON HER COUCH. He sat in the recliner, Twinky on his lap in a surprising show of affection. She barely let Grace touch her, but didn't hesitate jumping on Ryder. She didn't blame the cat. Ryder McKay was turning out to be an irresistible force, let's face it.

"She could use a bath," he remarked, but made no effort to remove her.

"You go right ahead," Grace told him. She would pay good money to see that. She was sore and annoyed that she'd gotten injured. She didn't like appearing weak. Especially in front of Ryder, for some reason. She wanted to wrap herself in her afghan and wallow a little over how the day had turned out. Which annoyed her further. She wasn't a wallower.

"Go away."

"I don't think so."

He wouldn't let her out of his sight. He'd barely let her take a shower, stayed standing in front of the bathroom door the whole time, asking her every five seconds if she was okay.

She closed her eyes. "Why can't you just leave me to my misery?"

"The E.R. doc wanted to keep you for observation. He only let you come home because I promised that I wouldn't leave you alone tonight."

"He won't know if you go."

"But I will."

She rolled her eyes. "Live wild. Break a few rules," she joked, but felt little humor. Her body ached all over.

He watched her with an unfathomable look on his face. He could be infuriatingly stubborn, she thought, and rolled on her side to turn her back on him, a move she immediately regretted when her bruised ribs protested.

The brace felt cumbersome on her ankle. The doc had insisted on that to give her stretched-out ligaments a chance to recover. Her banged-up shoulder ached. She allowed the tiniest of sighs but, of course, he heard it.

"You should take one of the pills they gave you."

"You should mind your own business," she called over her shoulder.

She'd chucked the pills into a kitchen drawer earlier. And she didn't plan on filling the additional prescription they'd given her.

"Ever thought about working on that prickly attitude? Sweeten that act of yours and you might get a boyfriend someday."

If getting the rolling pin from the kitchen wouldn't be so much trouble, she'd do it and beat him over the head. "Maybe I do have a boyfriend. How do you know I don't?"

"Not Dylan."

"You don't know that." She still wouldn't turn.

"He looked comfortable in your house the other day, but he walked away and left me here with you," he said in a thoughtful tone. "Either he's not your boyfriend, or he's stupid. He didn't look stupid."

"I could have a very serious relationship back in the city." She would someday. Maybe. When she got her act together. And whoever she chose was going to be way less irritating than Ryder McKay.

"I don't think so. Any decent man would have come here with you to say goodbye to your brother. And you had no emergency number listed on your medical record. I noticed that at the hospital."

The man's ability to be irritating was as vast as the borderlands. "Medical records are private," she pointed out.

"I saw them accidentally. It's not a crime to have good peripheral vision."

"I wonder if a person can be accidentally smothered with a throw pillow," she mused out loud as she turned back onto her back, adjusting said pillow, and settling into the most comfortable position under the circumstances.

He had the gall to grin.

Oh, God, not the dimples. She was in no shape to resist *those*. She needed to distract herself with something.

"How is Ray?" The man had been annoyed as hell by his injuries, but unfailingly polite to her.

"He's got a cast. Starting tomorrow, he'll be on permanent office duty."

Which seemed to please Ryder. Maybe it meant that he could spend more time in the field now, as opposed to at his office. She just hoped it'd be a field far away from her ranch.

He looked her over from top to bottom. "You look miserable."

"That kind of talk get you a lot of girls?"

"You'd be surprised." He flashed a quick, lethal grin. "I think I know what you need."

"A meteor to slice through the roof and take out the recliner you're sitting in?"

He gently placed the cat on the floor next to him then stood with a chiding expression, but didn't take the bait. "You need a hug."

She scowled. "I'm an army vet, not a teddy bear."

"I watch TV. I know these kinds of things. Women always want more hugs and jewelry. Makes them feel better. It's a genetic defect I'm willing to humor if it puts you to sleep." He strode toward her.

For real? She shrank to the back of the couch, which was the size of Texas. Her grandfather hadn't believed in small things. If only he'd also left an oversize baseball bat behind. Preferably, within reach.

But since she had no defensive weapons at hand, she steeled herself for the contact.

Instead of bending for a quick hug, Ryder lay down next to her and took her into his arms.

She held her body stiff. "That's a little too much." The words came out in an embarrassingly weak squeak.

"Anything worth doing, is worth doing right."

Sure, resort to platitudes. "Sexual harassment," she grumbled.

"No offense, but you don't look very sexy just now. I'm sure it'll come back. Not to worry," he added, his tone on the wrong side of patronizing.

She tried to sock him in the stomach, but he caught her hand.

"Let go," she snapped at him. "I'm not going to lie here with you holding hands."

"Will you lie here with me peacefully?"

She glared a couple of death rays at him, but then she rolled her eyes in capitulation. She was so sore all over, she didn't have the will to fight him.

"I have no idea who you are for real, you know that, right? Do you know how weird this is?"

"Feels okay from this end."

Was he flirting with her? "Cop a feel and lose the hand," she warned, just so they were clear.

"What happened to all that warm Texas hospitality?"

"What happened to respecting my personal space? Are you always this friendly with complete strangers?"

"We're not complete strangers. You saved my life. I saved yours. Unbreakable bonds and all that."

She groaned.

She needed something to distract her from his hard body. She might not have been at her all-time high on the sexy-meter, but he was at the top of the chart any old day. His body spoke to hers, even as bruised as she was, and her body answered.

She didn't like the things it was saying.

"Tell me something about yourself." Talking had to be better than to be lying there silently and wanting him.

"I'm third generation military. Grew up all over the world. Parents live in Seattle. Does that make you feel more comfortable with me?"

If only. While she was feeling all sorts of things, "comfortable" wasn't on the list.

"I have three sisters," he went on after a second. "Twin girls, sixteen, Lisa and Amanda. And Cheryl. She's twenty. They're pretty fantastic."

She tried to picture him handing out hugs and doing the brotherly thing. The image came pretty easily. He was as tough as they came, but he did have a gentleness at his core.

She thought of Tommy, glanced up at the urn on the mantel, and decided that her brother would have liked Ryder.

If only to annoy her.

That made her smile, and she relaxed enough to patiently wait two whole minutes. "Okay. Hug is over. I'm feeling much better." She gave him a little shove, which failed to budge him.

"This is so much more comfortable than the recliner," he mumbled against her hair, sounding half-asleep, which she was pretty sure he was faking.

For a second, she considered doing him serious bodily harm. She didn't. For one, she wasn't sure she could pull it off in her present condition. Two, being snuggled against him did feel comforting. Not that she would have admitted that even under threat of torture.

Months had passed since she'd last hugged Tommy. It'd been even longer since she'd had another man this close to her.

She closed her eyes. *Fine.* Just this once. "Don't think we're going to make a habit of this, city slicker," she warned him.

He simply drew her closer without saying anything.

Chapter Seven

Ryder woke to an earsplitting scream and Grace on top of him, trying to get him into a choke hold.

"Grace!" He grabbed her into a tight hug, then saw stars when she slammed her forehead into his nose.

Her knees were all over the place, too, so he rolled her under him and pinned her down before she could have done either of them serious injury.

"Grace," this time he whispered the word close to her ear.

And she went deadly still.

Enough moonlight came through the window so he could see her wild, wide-eyed stare as her brain adjusted to reality.

"I thought…" The words came out in a hoarse voice that gave him a glimpse into her past and broke his heart a little.

"You're safe. You're home." He loosened his hold on her. "It's okay."

He rolled off her and pushed off the couch. She didn't need to be crowded just now. But he didn't go too far. He leaned against the mantel and watched as she sat up, pulled up her knees and wrapped her arms around them.

She looked thoroughly embarrassed. "Did I hurt you?"

"You don't need to worry about me." He ignored his aching nose which felt as if it'd been driven up into his brain. She was a better fighter asleep than half the people he knew were when awake. Something to remember. "Bad dream?"

"Sometimes I can't tell the difference," she admitted after a minute.

He knew what she meant: the difference between the past and the present. A close friend had come back from Afghanistan with near-debilitating PTSD. It'd been two years and he was still a mess. All considered, Grace was dealing with her problems admirably.

"How about I bring you a glass of water?" He padded barefoot to the kitchen, around the table where she'd served him breakfast after that first night. She had a good heart. She was selfless, willing to go the extra mile for others. She was a fine woman.

He wouldn't have minded if the wife he found, when he found her, was a little like Grace Cordero. Not in everything, obviously. Grace was done with the fighting. She could never make it onto his team, and be his partner that way. Even if she wanted to try, she wouldn't be given a chance, not with PTSD. And she didn't want marriage, in any case. She'd been very clear about that.

But in other ways, she was all right to be around.

And she was sexy, he thought as he came back with the water and caught her stretching, standing by the couch. Her worn T-shirt stretched over amazing breasts, the hem pulling from her pants and revealing a flat, smooth stomach that sent need spiraling through him.

She seemed completely unaware of how good she

looked, had never once turned flirty with him or with anyone else that he had seen. She seemed too preoccupied with helping others to even be conscious of her body.

He was aware of it. More than aware. He raised his gaze to her face as he handed her the glass. "Drink."

She sat back down and took a long gulp, then another. Her shoulders relaxed. She breathed more evenly. It was like watching rippling water smooth out on the surface of a pond.

"Feeling better?"

She nodded. "Sorry."

He shrugged it off. "I'll be back asleep the second my head hits the pillow." He eyed the sofa.

But she rolled her neck as she stood and stepped away. "I'm going up to bed."

"I'm supposed to be sticking close to you."

"Nice try, city slicker." She walked to the stairs, looked toward the window. "It's almost morning. I'm fine."

He wanted to argue with that, but she was the medical professional.

"I could go up with you. Sit in a chair, whatever."

"Take the sofa. You need some decent sleep."

He would have rather slept next to her. He caught the thought and turned it around in his head a few times while she plodded up the stairs. Liking her company too much would lead to no good. Grace Cordero wasn't the woman of his plans. Starting something with her would make no sense whatsoever.

So he simply watched as she climbed the stairs, wincing with pain now and then, and he resisted taking her into his arms and carrying her up there. When she disappeared down the hallway, he lay back on the sofa and closed his eyes.

And missed her next to him.

Ryder drew a deep, slow breath. The sooner he found that wife, the better.

She woke to knocking on the front door, and stumbled down the stairs half-asleep just in time to see Ryder letting Dylan in. The hard look of hate that crossed Dylan's face was new. It quickly disappeared once he spotted her.

"I heard you got hurt yesterday. Just wanted to see if there's anything I can do to help." He stepped forward and held out a plate covered in aluminum wrap. "Molly sent some hot breakfast. She'll be over to check on you later. How is the foot?"

"Thank you." She took the plate and limped to the kitchen, wishing she'd gotten up earlier and had at least combed her hair. "Nothing serious. Ankle popped out, got popped back in. Hate the brace."

"Glad to see you're wearing it, anyway," Dylan said, as both men followed her.

Ryder was all cleaned up, she noticed, and fully dressed. He'd probably been waiting for her to wake up so he could leave. She thought of the way they'd spent the first half of the night, together on the couch, and her body warmed at the memory.

And then Dylan hugged her suddenly, as she put the plate on the counter. She didn't resist. But neither did she feel any of the sexual awareness she'd felt in Ryder's arms.

She stepped away to get a fork, but didn't touch the food. She could never eat first thing in the morning. She needed coffee. "Tell Molly I really appreciate this." She went to set up the pot and realized she was out of filters.

Shoot me now.

"So what happened? I hear they found a tunnel near the ravine."

She told Dylan what she knew. With all the emergency services out there yesterday, everyone probably already heard all about it.

Ryder's cell phone rang. He stepped outside to take it.

"Is he bothering you?" Dylan asked. "I don't like some government man snooping around your place. He has no right to be here. The tunnel had nothing to do with you. He's acting like you're under house arrest or something."

"He's just trying to help." She rolled her eyes. "He thinks he is, anyway. He only stayed the night because the doc in the E.R. said I might have a concussion."

"You could have called me." A touch of hurt in his voice.

"It was no big deal."

"Just watch him. That's all. He could be setting you up. They think illegal business is going on at your ranch. He's cozying up to you. He's in your house all the time, without as much as a search warrant. He could be building a case against you. I know you know him from the army, but…you have to question this guy's motivation."

She thought for a second. What if Dylan was right? How well did she know Ryder, anyway? It's not as if she'd never met government men who were less than honest, who skirted the truth to achieve their agenda.

Something she needed to think about.

Among other things.

She faced Dylan. "I've been meaning to ask you.

Where do the men you bring in camp exactly? I didn't see any sign of them yesterday."

"At the far end of the ravine. They had a good time, too. They'll be coming back. Here." He pulled out his cell phone and scrolled through some pictures of people in fatigues rappelling down a rock face that she recognized. "The trainer sent these over with a new reservation."

He shook his head. "Don't see the attraction, personally. Staying out there in that heat with no running water but, hey, if they're into that kind of stuff, I'm happy to take the money."

Part of which went to her, she thought, and helped her keep the ranch until she decided what to do with it. "I'm glad you found a use for the place," she said. "Border patrol might want to talk to you about those team building people, though. They might have seen something."

He put away the phone. "I doubt it. If they did, why wouldn't they tell me, or the authorities? I'm guessing the smugglers were smart enough to move only in between groups, when they were sure no one was out there."

Or only on dark, starless nights.

"Makes no sense. Why the ravine? Has to be the hardest place to build a tunnel, through all that rock. There are plenty of places along the border where it'd be easy digging."

Dylan thought for a moment. "Probably that's why. They knew nobody would be looking there. Drug running is a billion-dollar business from what I hear. They can afford fancy equipment to do the hard work. Kenny said the tunnel even had ventilation and electricity."

She hadn't heard that. Ryder had probably dragged

her off to the E.R. by the time that was discovered. "I hate this."

"I know. I wish you didn't get involved." A troubled expression crossed his face. "You didn't need this, with everything that happened with Tommy recently and all that."

Ryder strode back in, a frown on his face. "I need to go into Hullett."

"Me, too." Grace immediately stepped toward him. If there'd been some development in the Molinero case, she didn't want to miss it. And if he was trying to pin the smuggling on her... Wasn't there a saying about keeping one's friends close, but keeping one's enemy's closer?

"I think I'm going to fill that prescription. My ankle is still throbbing," she told him.

"You should stay here and keep off that foot. I'll stay with you," Dylan offered and took her hand. "I can call Molly to go to town and fill that prescription."

Ryder's lips narrowed. "Actually, this errand I need to run... I could probably use her help."

She pulled away from Dylan, grabbed the plate and put it into the fridge, then limped toward the stairs. "Give me a minute to get ready." And left the men staring daggers at each other in her kitchen.

They both moved at the same time to help her up the stairs.

She flashed them a forbidding look over her shoulder. "Don't even think about it." She wasn't an invalid, dammit.

She made it up on her own, brushed her teeth, washed her face, changed out of her wrinkled clothes. She'd taken a quick shower the night before, after Ryder had driven her home from the E.R., but had put regular clothes on instead of pajamas, to feel more comfortable around him.

As if that was a possibility. Her awareness of him seemed impossible to shake.

She limped down the stairs, and tripped halfway. Ryder was there before she could have fallen, and carried her the rest of the way in his arms. He'd showered last night, too, and was still wearing his own jeans, but the clean shirt she'd given him from Tommy's belongings. And the cowboy boots, of course. Sans spurs.

He was learning.

"Dylan said to tell you goodbye for him. He had some pressing appointment," Ryder said.

She didn't mind. She didn't like the tension between the two men. It was silly and unnecessary.

"Where are we going?" she asked, stepping into her own boots. Right foot only. The brace on her injured ankle wouldn't allow for shoes for a while.

"Stakeout." He hesitated. "Unless you're not up to it. I could drop you at a girlfriend's house."

"Not a chance." She put out fresh water and food for Twinky and the kittens who, thank God, were old enough for solids, then stepped outside and locked the front door behind them.

She realized her truck was still out by the ravine. Great.

"We would have taken my SUV, anyway." Ryder apparently read her thoughts.

Of course they would have. Because he just had to be in charge. She limped away from him. "I have to take care of the horses."

"I already walked Cookie. Not because I didn't think you could handle it. I like the old gal."

Had she been that prickly about accepting help? Okay, fine, she had. "Thanks. I appreciate it."

He'd gone out of his way to help, and then went the extra mile to make sure he didn't hurt her feelings. If she didn't watch it, she was going to start to like him. Which would be really stupid.

Dylan was right. She would be smart to be cautious of Ryder McKay.

She walked into the barn, breathing in the familiar scents of horses and hay and felt immediately at home, relaxed a little. Cookie and Maureen snorted a greeting.

There'd be no more riding for her now, she thought with regret, and patted them, checking Cookie's side. "How are you this morning? Looking good." She'd always talked to animals.

Cookie's stomach was no longer distended. She'd be going back home soon. Murray was being let out of the hospital today to recover from all the testing and the minor surgery he'd ended up needing.

She went for fresh water first. "Where did you put the bucket?"

"Never touched it," he called over his shoulder, busy mucking out Cookie's stall.

She spotted the damned thing in the corner and limped toward it. She noticed a couple of other things out of place, too. Ryder must have been looking around for something this morning.

Searching the place? She watched him when he wasn't looking. But he seemed to be paying attention to only the horses, immersed in what he was doing. He insisted on helping with the water and the feed, so they were done in under ten minutes. Which didn't lessen her annoyance of him messing with her things and possibly spying.

"So where are we going exactly?" she asked as she closed the barn and they began to walk toward his car. Ryder slowed his steps so she could keep up with him.

"Staking out the wire mill. One of the women rescued from the tunnel last night says she was told she could get a job there if she could make her way over."

"They don't hire a lot of women."

"Exactly."

According to Esperanza, Paco had been hired by the wire mill, too. "Doesn't mean they have anything to do with anything. Could be whoever is bringing these people over is using the mill as bait. It's one of the largest employers around here. Everyone has heard of it. Makes the bad guys sound legit."

She thought about that some more. "I thought the mill had been cleared. I didn't think you found anything that linked them to Paco."

"When I called, I was told nobody there had any contact with a Paco Molinero. Checked with HR. Checked with the managers. They aren't hiring at all, supposedly, haven't for a while, not in this economy."

She hated the thought that anyone at the mill could have something to do with illegal business. She knew a couple of guys there.

They talked about that, among other things, on the ride on the way over.

"So if you all think the mill is somehow involved in something shady, how come immigration services is not swarming the place?"

"Not enough evidence," he said without looking at her.

She thought about that for a second, about him, his buddies, how he'd come to be on her land. "I don't think so. They search places based on rumor. One anonymous tip comes in over the phone, and there they go."

Sending one man on a stakeout instead of a full INS team that could lock the place down and ID every worker didn't make any sense.

"INS does what INS does. I don't work for them."

"Who do you work for, exactly?"

He didn't say anything.

"You never wear a uniform with any kind of identifying insignia on it. Neither do your friends."

His jaw tightened.

"You're in some sort of a special unit." She shared her conclusion with him. "But I don't think it has to do with budgetary recommendation."

He remained silent.

"Obviously, you can't talk about it." She thought some more. "Because what you're doing is top secret."

He stared straight ahead.

"I have nothing to do with the smuggling."

He did look at her then, annoyance flashing across his face. "I know you don't. Give me some credit."

He did sound sincere.

"If I thought you were involved, you'd be in an interrogation room right now, not riding shotgun, going on a stakeout with me. You're all right."

"How do you know?"

"Over a decade of experience. Plus I ran you through the system."

She hated the thought of that, but liked that he admitted it. "I don't know who I can trust."

"You can trust me."

She had instincts, too. Honed in battle. They said he was a dangerous man. Yet she didn't think he was a danger to her.

They reached town and he pulled into the drive-through of the first fast-food restaurant they came across. He bought her coffee.

"Thanks." Something warm and fuzzy was happening in her chest. She ignored it. She wasn't ready to let the subject of his team go just yet.

"I don't think you're here about some poor guy who comes up to do farmwork for three dollars an hour," she said once she had the first few sips of hot liquid. "The six of you are here to fry bigger fish."

He cast her a fathomless glance. "Think about something else."

Okay, really big fish. "I'm thinking your mission has to do with national security. You're waiting for something. What is it?"

"For your own good, you should stop guessing."

Which meant she was getting uncomfortably close. "This has to do either with terrorists, or some nasty weapon coming through."

A muscle began jumping in his cheek.

Her eyes went wide. "Both?"

He swore under his breath. "Do you ever listen?"

She smirked at him. "Only when people tell me things I want to hear."

"We're not going to discuss this any further."

"I have no intention to pump you for details. I do understand concepts like undercover op and national security." Not that she believed in unlimited government power. But she really was beginning to believe that Ryder was working here on the side of good. If she didn't, she wouldn't be helping him.

They reached the mill and she turned her attention to that. The parking lot had a gate, but it stood open, nobody at the guardhouse. The place wasn't exactly a high-security facility. Ryder pulled in, parked in the back, in a spot from where they could see the front door and people coming and going.

He got a fancy camera with a telephoto lens from the backseat and took some pictures, then lowered the expensive equipment to his lap. "Do you know how to use one of these?"

She'd used cameras before. Even nice ones. "I'm sure I could figure it out."

"We'll do a little surveillance before I go in." He held the camera out for her. "Don't touch the settings and you'll be fine."

Their fingers brushed together as she took the camera, the brief connection sending tingles zinging through her. Which reminded her again how he'd held her in his arms part of the night. Which brought on more tingles.

Ridiculous.

She refused to have the hots for Ryder McKay. She was a woman with principles. He was annoying, bossy and inconvenient in her life in every way. He was a *government man.* She deliberately let her mind linger on that thought, but it failed to produce the usual cutting distaste.

He pushed the door open. "You keep taking pictures. I'll go and look around."

"I'm sorry. Did I miss the memo that said you were the boss of Texas? Sometimes papers get shuffled around on my desk."

He looked at her with incredulity in his eyes. Then the look hardened. "You were almost killed yesterday. You're not coming with me. No way. End of story."

"I can handle whatever you can handle," she shot back, although she wasn't sure if the words were true. But she didn't want him to see her as a weak mess.

"I can't afford to have to worry about you."

Blunt. Okay, that hurt. So this was it. He'd seen her have that night terror. And now he knew she was broken. Now he knew she was good for nothing. Her eyes burned suddenly. She bit the inside of her cheek and looked out the side window. Shrugged. "Whatever."

He hesitated, watching her, but she didn't turn back to him again.

He got out. The door closed behind him. She didn't even watch him walk away.

By the time she figured out the camera, he was across the parking lot and walking around the corner of the building. A couple of guys stood around, talking. She snapped pictures and felt ridiculous. A large percentage of the workforce was Hispanic, but they were from the local community. She even knew some of them. Spying on them felt wrong.

She found a new one in her zoom, Jesus, who rented an apartment from her old pastor at the Methodist church, then realized the man was heading straight toward her. She put the camera down before he could have caught her taking pictures. He walked to his rust-eaten truck one row in front of hers, spotted her, waved with a big smile and came over.

She got out. "Hey."

"What are you doing here, chica? Long time no see. Ready to give my jalapeño chili another try?" Dust and dirt covered him. The place had shower facilities, but they were so filthy, most of the workers waited until they were home to get clean. Jesus was a tinner last time she'd heard, working over molten tin, coating wires, pretty much the sweatiest job at the mill.

"As soon as my stomach lining grows back." She wished she had her pickup with the cooler in the back so she could offer him a cold drink.

"You here looking for a hot guy to take home? I could introduce you to a couple."

"Only if he's willing to muck out my stalls."

He gave a wicked grin. "Is that what they call it these days?"

She punched him in the shoulder. "Get your mind out of the gutter."

"Maria likes it there." He winked at her. He was the content husband of a pretty woman and the happy father of three kids. "Who are you waiting for, anyway?"

"A friend is dropping off an application. I'm just along for the ride." Great. Now she was lying to her friends.

Jesus took in the fancy SUV. "Manager man?"

She nodded.

"No hiring, for nobody. A ten heads operator left last month—they're not even replacing him."

She actually knew what that meant. Tommy had done a brief stint as a ten heads operator back in the day, working in the drawing room, working on the machine that ran ten strands of wire, drawing them down to a smaller size.

"The mill can't be having money troubles. Old Mitzner seems to be doing good." She nodded toward the sparkling new BMW in the owner's spot by the door.

"That's Mikey's. He took over when his father died last year."

She stared. Old Mitzner was gone, and nobody had told her. Of course, she'd been too busy with her job, with her classes and Tommy. Still. She took a slow breath. Even Dylan hadn't said anything. He probably assumed she'd already heard.

She stared at the building. Mitzner could be an ornery old coot, but he was a decent man. He always did right by his workers. His son, Mikey, was a weasel.

"Sorry to hear that," she said. "Maybe Mikey will grow up to the task."

Jesus shrugged. "Machines are down half the time. He won't put money into repair. Customers are leaving. They can get the same job done south of the border cheaper. If he shuts down the place…" He shook his head.

"He won't," she rushed to reassure the man. They couldn't. The mill employed probably half of the unskilled labor force in Hullett. If the mill closed, the town would collapse.

"God willing." Jesus nodded.

"Do you hang much with newcomers these days?" she asked.

"At church. A lot fewer people come across than used to. Tough to find jobs these days."

"Have you run into anyone by the name of Paco Molinero?"

"Never heard of him? Why?"

"Friend of a friend."

He nodded. "Are you staying for good this time?"

"A couple of days. I brought Tommy's ashes back."

Jesus's face turned somber. "I'm sorry about your brother. He was a good man."

"Thank you. Say hi to Maria and the kids for me." She liked Maria, a bright young woman, kindergarten teacher and a volunteer at the retirement nursing home. She'd even helped out with Tommy at the end.

Jesus gave her a parting smile, then went back to his business of getting home to his wife and children.

After he left, Grace snapped a few more pictures, catching Mikey Mitzner coming out in a thousand-dollar suit. The motor of the BMW roared to life, and it peeled away from its spot, looking out of place among the rows of cars, most of which looked ready for the junkyard.

But if the mill was doing so badly, where had Mikey's fancy car come from? He had no income that she knew of, save the mill. He'd never put himself out in school. His father's money had pushed him through college, but he'd come back home right after, never worked anywhere but on the top floor of the mill, in the management offices.

An issue she wanted to discuss with Ryder, but Lord knew where Ryder had gone off to. And this was prime opportunity that shouldn't be wasted. Mikey was out. His office would be empty. If he made his money from something other than the mill…say dabbling in human trafficking…

Anger flooded her at the thought and pushed her from the car. She left the camera inside—the tele-photo lens would have made her too conspicuous—and flipped the lock before she closed the door behind her.

Ryder was probably going to be mad at her. She paused. Then shrugged as she started out toward the mill. She wanted to see Mikey's office without Mikey in it, and this was her chance.

She hurried toward the front door, tucking her neck in, trying not to limp, trying to look like one of the secretaries, the few women who worked here.

Sneak in, find proof of wrongdoing, sneak back out before Ryder figured out that she was missing. Piece of cake.

Chapter Eight

The workers used the back entry. Since she needed to get to the offices, Grace went in through the front.

Daisy Webster sat in her chair for once, instead of chasing after another man on the factory floor. She looked up from her web surfing just in time to notice Grace. She wore some fancy fashion top with an asymmetric neck that plunged way too low. Rumor had it her fashion addiction usually took more than one man to support.

"Hey, there, Gracie." The greeting rang out in a cool tone. Daisy had endlessly chased after Tommy back in the day. Tommy had never paid her any attention, which earned a good deal of resentment from Daisy after a while, and that resentment had spread to include Grace. "Who are you looking for?"

She would have preferred sneaking up the staircase without anyone noticing her, but there was no way to do that.

"Bobbi Marzec." She said the first name that popped into her head, loudly—even out here, you could hear the machines. Bobbi kept the office computers in shape and he'd been one of Tommy's friends.

"Is he expecting you?"

"He wants to buy Tommy's dirt bike." She stuck with the truth while going around the question.

Daisy shrugged then went back to her computer, probably scanning online deals on fashion and fashion accessories. Grace headed up the stairs, hurrying.

The mill offices sprawled on the top floor of the flat, three-story building. She passed several people on her way up, but didn't know any of them. There'd obviously been some turnover since old man Mitzner had died. Mikey probably brought his own cronies on board, people who gave him their undivided loyalty and admiration, agreeing with all his ideas wholeheartedly.

His father had a couple of tough old bird managers. Mikey wouldn't like that, she thought, and her suspicions were confirmed as she walked by a row of offices, all with new faces behind the desk. The average managerial age had dropped at least twenty years since she'd last been here.

Bobbi's office was in the left wing of the top floor. She'd have to go there, too, at one point. In case Daisy asked him how the dirt bike deal went. But first she wanted to check out Mikey's office; she had no idea how long he'd be gone.

She went straight to the back. Nobody paid her much attention. Then her luck ran out. The door wouldn't budge when she twisted the knob. If this was a movie, she'd pull some pins from her hair and would be inside under a minute, she thought. But her short hair didn't need pins, and she wasn't exactly comfortable with breaking and entering.

She looked through the glass, but didn't see anything suspicious inside: shelves, stacks of paper, a laptop in the center of the desk. No big sign on the wall that said, I Smuggle Drugs, or, I Support Illegal Immigration.

Maybe she should wait until Mikey came back. She could then get into his office with some trumped-up excuse, look around surreptitiously while distracting him with some chatter. Although, what they could chat about escaped her. Neither she, nor Tommy had ever been friends with him.

Dylan, she remembered suddenly. Dylan and Mikey had been on the high school football team together. Dylan because he'd had talent; Mikey because his father had bought the uniforms and most of the training equipment for the school.

Maybe she could ask Dylan if the guys from the team still hung out at Mimi's Bar and Grill. She could join them and get a feel for what kind of a man Mikey was these days. Dylan would be happy to take her along and reintroduce her to the old gang. Except she didn't want to deceive Dylan about yet another thing. She was already keeping secrets from him—and owed him a big apology when this was over.

She thought about shoving her shoulder against the door and simply pushing it in. But she had no idea how much noise that would make. Would the people sitting in the other offices hear her?

She was no longer at war. The laws of war no longer applied. So she decided to stop at breaking and entering. She rattled the knob one more time, cast one last forlorn look at the locked office, then walked away. She hoped Ryder gained more useful information than she did. She walked past a young cleaning woman who was emptying the garbage cans. The woman scurried out of her way.

She was Hispanic. So were a lot of other people in Hullett. She wore a turtleneck shirt, which was kind of strange. Not many people in South Texas wore turtlenecks, not in over one-hundred-degree weather. Then she realized why this one did, as she caught a glimpse of what looked like burn scars visible from the top.

But it wasn't the scar that piqued Grace's interest. What made her take a second look was the woman's skittish, beaten dog body language.

Her eyes wouldn't meet Grace's. So she watched the woman for a few minutes as she moved from desk to desk, neck pulled in, eyes nervously darting around without making any eye contact with anyone.

She'd seen women like that before, both in the States and during her overseas tours of duty—women who lived under threat of violence, who went to great lengths to become invisible. And this one seemed to be especially good at it. The few people in the offices and cubicles paid scant attention to her.

She was watchful, aware of her environment to the extreme, so only a few minutes passed before she caught Grace watching her. She startled, tucked her neck in and hurried toward the staircase with a worried look on her face, her cart rattling as she pushed it with increasing speed.

Instinct drew Grace after her.

The woman abandoned her cart on the landing at the top of the staircase and ran down. Probably illegal, Grace thought, taking her for INS. With the brace on her foot, she could never catch up with the woman, so Grace resorted to her best military voice. "Stop right there!"

The woman froze and shrank. Turned slowly, and

waited with her arms wrapped around her slight body while Grace hobbled over.

"Why are you running from me?"

Despair washed over her face. "No prison, *por favor*." Her eyes filled with tears. "I just want to go home. No prison, *señora*. Por favor."

"I'm not with the police." She stepped back to give her some space. "I'm not here for you. I just want to ask questions."

The woman rubbed her tears away with the back of her hand, and looked at her with mistrust. "All good girls. Everybody wants to go home. No prison," she said in pretty good, if halting, English.

Somebody had obviously threatened her with prison and had succeeded well with the intimidation. Being locked up seemed to be the only thing the woman could think of.

Everybody, she had said.

"No prison." Grace drew a deep breath as a tractor trailer pulling up to the loading docks outside caught her attention for a second. "I'm here to help. Where are the others?"

The woman inched back. She glanced at the brace on Grace's foot. She knew that she could outrun Grace, but the fear still held her in place.

"No prison," Grace repeated. She reached into her pocket for her phone. Then she changed her mind and left it where it was. A call might scare off the woman altogether. She might think that Grace was calling in the reinforcements. Better see first if there really was something to call Ryder about. "I want to help you."

The woman hesitated another moment, then seemed to have come to some sort of decision. She hurried back up to her cart and grabbed a two-liter soda bottle filled with water then came back to Grace. She glanced around, nearly vibrating with nervous energy, then hurried down the next flight of stairs, but holding back enough so Grace could follow her.

She ducked through a door with a sign that warned *Employees Only,* hurried along a dark and narrow hallway without windows, then into another staircase that went down and down. Then when they ran out of stairs, she pushed through the last door into some sort of a basement.

Low ceilings, cobwebs, old fallen beams, rats scurrying along the walls. A single lightbulb hung from a wire in the middle of the ceiling, illuminating a twenty-foot-wide circle while leaving the rest of the creepy place shrouded in darkness.

A sense of unease swept through Grace, a premonition that they weren't alone. The short hairs at the back of her neck rose suddenly.

The woman stepped forward, into the circle of light. Held back by instinct, Grace remained in the shadows.

"Qué pasa?" came the challenge from a dark corner, the man's voice cold and hard.

The woman answered in Spanish, and Grace understood enough to know that she'd said something about bringing water. The man yelled at her for not bringing beer.

He pulled a cord and turned on another light that illuminated him at last. He stood with his feet apart in front of a ratty old recliner that had stuffing hanging out the back. His clothes rumpled, he rubbed his eyes and stretched. He must have been sleeping in the dark.

His short, dark hair stuck up in every direction, his fore-head low and decorated with an angry scar.

The woman tried to skirt around him as she got closer, but he grabbed her and fondled her roughly as he took the bottle from her. He let loose a cruel laugh as she tried to get away, his lips curling into a sneer.

Grace's hands fisted at her side. She noted the distance between them, the fact that the man had a gun tucked into his belt. She moved forward, then stopped as the idiot let his prey go at last.

It seemed he wasn't serious about doing harm to the woman, at least not this time. He lifted the bottle to his lips to drink. The woman scurried back to the stairs and ran up. Grace could hear as the door closed behind her at the top.

Okay. Now what?

She was about to follow, not fully understanding why she'd been brought here, when the man lowered the bottle and took a few steps toward the back wall, to a wooden door she hadn't seen before. He unlocked the door and tossed the bottle of water inside.

She caught a glimpse of what looked like a prison cell, an impression of blinking faces, red eyes, stringy unwashed hair, thin bodies covered in rags. The closest thing she could liken it to was a painting she'd seen on a school field trip a million years ago, about the hold of a slave ship.

He slammed the door shut with a bang and turned the key. Then he sat back into his recliner and pulled out a tattered copy of a magazine and began to flip through it. She couldn't make out any of the writing from where she stood, but could see that the pages contained mostly nudity. Which didn't bode well for the women locked up inside. And explained why they would draw back when the door opened, instead of rushing forward.

Grace drew a slow breath and assessed the situation, careful to remain in the deep shadows as she skirted the lit areas, picking her steps carefully in the dark. She needed to get out of here and call Ryder. He had to get his team over here.

She made it over to the dark stairs, crept up without making any noise, her heart beating in her ear, sweat beading on her brow. An eternity seemed to pass before she made it to the top. Her hand was on the door handle when it was yanked open from the outside. Another scruffy man stood in front of her, his eyes narrowing.

"What the hell are you doing here?" he asked and without waiting for an answer, kicked her down the stairs.

She wasn't in the car.

Maybe she went for a walk to stretch her legs. Or could be she got tired of waiting for him and caught a ride with a friend, Ryder thought, but his instincts said otherwise. He was pretty sure she would have at least given him a call to let him know not to wait for her.

The most likely explanation, and also his least favorite, was that she'd gotten tired of waiting and had come after him. But why didn't she call? Maybe she was in a situation where she couldn't. He didn't like the thought.

He leaned against the SUV and looked toward the building. The heat was stifling, the air dry. He wanted a cold drink, but that would have to wait.

To call her or not was the question. If she was snooping around somewhere in there, the phone's ringing could call attention to her. Then again, she was a smart one. Smart enough to turn her phone off if the situation called for it.

Her number was in his address book, so he selected it and pushed the green button. The call did ring out. But instead of Grace, a man's surly voice spoke on the other end, with a heavy accent. "Who the hell is this?"

Ryder slammed the phone closed and ran toward the building.

TWO AGAINST ONE. They were stronger and unbruised, while her recent injuries still ached all over. Grace fought for her life, holding nothing back. She ducked. Punched. Punched again. Kicked.

"Stop!"

They ignored her, of course. But she made another play for time, anyway. "I'm just looking for a friend. I just want to talk."

But they didn't seem in a talkative mood.

Her top-notch military training came in handy, especially since the other two were street fighters, fighting mean and dirty. They came at her at the same time, giving her no respite. Still, she could have probably handled them if the brace didn't throw her off balance.

One tripped her at the end, and she crashed to the hard ground. The next second they were both on top of her.

Pain sliced through her ribs, bringing back memories from the battlefield. She couldn't allow herself to be captured again. She fought like a cornered animal, blind now with fear as the past and the present overlapped in her mind. *I'm home. This is different.*

But terror overrode her brain.

Her attackers took full advantage.

Boots connected with her side, her chest, knocking the air out of her.

"Who are you? Why are you here?" This guy, the newcomer, didn't have an accent. He sounded like a local boy, but she didn't recognize him.

She pressed her lips together and waited curled in a ball until they were done with her. She wasn't going to fight her way out of this basement, not when either of them could pull a gun at any time and shoot her in the head. The key was to stay alive long enough for Ryder to find her.

He'd called. At least, she hoped it'd been him on the phone a minute ago. Then he would know she was in trouble.

Rough hands grabbed her, picked her up. One of the men opened the door on the back wall, the other one tossed her into the holding cell where she lay at last, exhausted and defeated, in a heap.

For a long minute, she could hear nothing but her own labored breathing. Then someone held a water bottle to her lips. She couldn't see anything in the dark, but she'd caught a long-enough glimpse before to know who she shared the cell with.

Someone whispered a few words to her in rushed Spanish.

"No habla Español. Lo siento," she whispered back.

Small hands tugged her farther from the door. Voices conversed in hurried whispers, so low they were barely a breath.

"Who are you?" she asked the darkness. "How many people are there here?"

A few whispered names. One who spoke English said, "Seven."

She sat up gingerly, gritting her teeth against the pain. "Why?"

Silence followed, then, "We were sold to a man here."

Okay, she knew stuff like that happened. But coming face-to-face with it, in her hometown, made her stomach constrict into a cold ball. Maybe something like this had happened to Paco.

"Have you met a man, Paco Molinero?" She'd only seen women here, but maybe there were men, too, and children, held at different locations. Maybe Paco had been sold, too, had escaped and had been shot for his bravery.

Nobody answered. She guessed that would be a no.

"What will they do to us?" she asked next.

"We don't know, *señora,*" the girl said after a few seconds, her voice small. "The men come—they take three or four. The women never come back. They're probably taken to work."

Forced prostitution, Grace thought, but didn't say anything.

She scooted back until she reached the wall and leaned her back against it. The small space smelled like sweat and dirt. "How long have you been here?"

"Two months."

She swallowed hard. She couldn't imagine two months in this dungeon, without light or fresh air, with barely enough room to move around.

"Is Paco your husband?" the girl asked her.

"Friend of a friend. I'm looking for his children, Miguel and Rosita."

"Miguel y Rosita?" someone whispered from the corner, followed by a couple of other words Grace didn't understand.

"Sí, los niños," the English-speaking girl answered, then listened to a rushed explanation, before saying in English, "Marianna has seen them."

Hope speared through Grace while the two women exchanged a few more sentences. "The children are at the train station. Marianna was first taken there before they brought her here."

"Edinburg?" Hullett didn't have a train station.

But the woman couldn't give her an answer. She probably had no idea where exactly she'd been.

Grace rubbed her hands over her face in the darkness, doing her best to think. If the children had been at a train station that meant they were kept on the move. They could be anywhere by now. She tried not to get discouraged. "When?"

The question was translated, as was the answer. "Last week."

More information came in Spanish, and that, too, was translated in whispers. "They're waiting for their adoption papers to be forged. The man there told Marianna that older girls like her, only bring maybe five thousand dollars. But young children can be adopted out for as much as twenty or thirty thousand."

And the twins, sold separately, would bring a small fortune, going to an unsuspecting American family who would think that they were dealing with a legitimate adoption organization. Anger rushed through Grace. She thought of Esperanza, desperately waiting for news on her family back at home, and felt sick to her stomach.

She tried to focus on her rage instead of the memories that being in a dark dungeon brought back. It worked for a while. But the claustrophobic darkness and heat, the smell of unwashed bodies, the nearly palpable fear in the air got to her eventually. Her nerves short-circuited.

Always at the worst time.

She curled into a ball as tremors shook her, breathless panic filling her, squeezing her chest. *Don't lose it now. Hold it together.*

Sweat rolled down her face as gruesome images flashed through her brain. She could hear the women whispering to each other, as if from a distance. She did her best to slow her breathing, to fill her lungs, but her lungs were drawn too tight.

Do what you're supposed to.

She'd been given tools to deal with this. So she tried to imagine her messed-up emotions as a rolling ocean, waves crashing violently, frighteningly on the surface. And she pictured herself, her core, as a whale deep below those waves. She was safe; she was peaceful under all that water. She could see the storm, but the storm couldn't touch her.

She had no idea how much time passed before her mind finally quieted and her breathing evened. She felt limp with exhaustion. The flashbacks and the panic attack were worse than the beating she'd received. At least the beating didn't make her feel as if something was wrong with her mind.

"Drink, *señora*." The water was offered to her again.

They didn't have enough water to start with. Seven women occupied the small cell. They had to ration that water, no doubt about it, make it last maybe as long as a full day. Yet when she politely refused, they urged her to drink.

So she did. The sooner she regained her strength a little, the sooner she could see about getting out of here.

She drank, then assessed her injuries and stretched her limbs to keep her muscles from stiffening up.

Half an hour passed before she felt semirecovered. It was as good as she was going to get. The longer she stayed the better the chance for another beating, or worse. If she were to escape, now was the time to do something about it.

She drew a deep breath, hoping she could sound confident enough to convince the others. "We're going to break out."

Her interpreter translated.

The silence that followed was deafening.

Then she heard a quiet sobbing.

"We don't want to go to prison," the woman said. "If anyone finds out that we're here, we go to prison. And if we don't earn back the money the man paid for us, they'll kill our families back home." The fear was palpable in her voice.

And no matter what Grace said after that, she couldn't convince the women to assist her in any kind of escape attempt. She couldn't really blame them. They'd been thoroughly intimidated and abused. They weren't trained soldiers.

But she was, still, in her heart, despite all her weaknesses. So she planned.

The faint line of light under the door had gone dark a while ago. The guard outside had probably gone back to sleep. The other one had left a while back, from what she could hear. Grace had to feel around in the dark to find the lock, memorize how high it was.

"I'm going to come back for you and get you out of here," she promised in a low whisper.

Since she wouldn't be able to deliver a strong enough

kick while balancing on her bad leg, she reclined in front of the door and supported herself with a knee and her hands as she kicked as hard as possible.

And the door did bounce open, just a plain wood panel made of two-by-fours, old with age. The men probably never imagined that the women would have the temerity to try to break out.

She rolled to her feet with a battle cry. The element of surprise was on her side. She knew roughly where the recliner was and threw herself on it, on top of the man who must have been in the process of jumping up, because they smacked their heads together and swore in unison, one in English, the other one in Spanish.

She blindly searched for his weapon while her head swam from the impact. Knocked his hand aside. Found the gun. Brought it up hard, and it connected with something with a sickening crunch. Probably the man's skull, as he suddenly went limp against her.

She shrugged him off.

"You're free," she called back to the women, searching for the light cord blindly, finding it by sheer luck. She yanked it hard and the light blinded her for a moment as it came on. She squinted her eyes. "Come on!"

The girls crowded up against the opening of the cell, but not one of them would set foot outside. They were holding their hands before their eyes.

She grabbed the interpreter by the arm. "Come on. Run!"

But they shrank back instead.

"*Señora,* no. We'll be punished. Come back, *señora.*"

Their fear was too strong. They'd been so abused, they no longer believed that freedom was possible.

"This is not over. I'll bring help." She turned to run. "Don't go anywhere with anyone until I come back."

But as she reached the staircase, the door on top opened, the silhouette of a man filling it. *Oh, God. Not again.*

She lifted her weapon, but his was already drawn.

Chapter Nine

Finding her came down to sheer luck, a fact that scared the soul out of Ryder. He'd been searching the building and happened to see a scared Mexican woman scurrying down the hallway. If there was trouble in here, she'd seen it, he thought.

The woman nearly fainted when Ryder confronted her, but he made her give up her story, and directions to the basement where she'd last seen Grace. Then he ran, ready to kill.

Except, the first person he saw when he kicked the door open, gun in hand, was Grace. "Don't shoot! It's me."

She leaned against the wall in a way he didn't like. Like they had hurt her. Hot fury pumped through his veins.

He raced down to her, taking the stairs two at a time. "Are you okay?"

"You have to call immediately. There are people here who need our help. I have some news on the children, too. They were last seen at a train station. Probably Edinburg."

She explained everything in a rush. He called even as he ran up to lock the door from the inside. He went back down and brought up some boards he saw in a heap in the corner, barricaded the door before he returned to her.

She was tying up a half-conscious man. About a half-dozen scruffy young women peered from behind a door in the wall behind her.

"Take it easy. They're scared to death," Grace warned him.

He wanted to grab her and check over every inch of her, but she was standing, apparently without major injury, and knowing that had to be enough for him at the moment. They were far from safe.

He turned his attention to the women. Man, they looked to be in bad shape. The urge to kick the bastard on the ground came on pretty strong, but he resisted it. A display of violence wouldn't be exactly reassuring for these people.

He took a second to calm his temper. "I'm with the United States government. I'm here to help you. Stay where you are. Stay down. Don't be afraid," he told the women in Spanish, the sight of them twisting his gut.

"You should go in there with them and close the door," he told Grace. "Barricade it from the inside in case the bad guys get here before reinforcements," he added, noticing suddenly that she was shaking. "Are you injured? Grace?"

"It's this place." Her voice was a strained whisper. She wrapped her arms around herself, a look of determination on her face.

"Did anyone hurt you?" Cold anger bubbled up inside him all over again as he gave her disheveled appearance a more careful look in the dim light, looking for new injuries.

She rocked herself. "Just give me a minute." And then she took some huge, heaving breaths, mumbling about water and whales.

But she kept hold of her gun, and when a minute later someone banged on the door at the top of the stairs, she immediately swung the weapon in the right direction.

She earned his profound respect while simultaneously activating all his protective instincts. She was driving him crazy. "Get back."

She ignored him, of course.

Giving in to her about little things had been a mistake. She had drawn the conclusion that they were some sort of partners.

"I'm the professional here. You're the civilian. Get back and take up a defensive position. That's an order."

But she just stood there, feet apart, a grim expression on her face, ready for anything.

He sure as hell wasn't. He wasn't at all ready for her to get hurt again, for example.

So when the bastards at the top of the stairs broke through the door, he rushed forward to make sure he would be between them and Grace.

Three men charged forward, all well-armed, shooting wildly in the dim space. The women screamed in the back.

He gritted his teeth and shot one of the men in the head, one in the chest, all while still dashing forward. By the time he could turn his attention to the third one, he was close enough so he could swing the butt of his gun up and smack the guy in the face, bringing him down.

If he could, he needed to keep alive as many as possible. His team needed information. These men were their first real break.

He kicked the guy's weapon away and kept his own gun aimed at the man's chest while he glanced back over his shoulder at Grace. "Did you get hit?"

She still held her gun, absolute fury on her face. The kind of fury that made him wish he had on a bulletproof vest under his shirt.

She lowered the weapon at long last. "You stood directly between me and the attackers, completely blocking me," she hissed.

He'd never in his life wanted to kiss a woman as badly as he wanted to kiss Grace Cordero at that moment. He marshaled his self-control and pressed his lips together for a second, before he asked, "Did you get hit?"

"No!" she yelled at him. "What the hell was that? Were you out sick the day they taught teamwork? Do you even know what the word means?"

All that fire was just turning him on even more.

"We're not a team." He bent to the man and tied him up with his own belt then strode back to her. "You were consulting. That's now over."

No way would he put her in danger like this again. His heart had about stopped when the men had opened fire. She'd seen plenty of rough stuff in the past and clearly she still wasn't over it. Involving her at all had been an incredibly stupid thing to do. Her participation would end here.

He opened his mouth to tell her, then decided it could wait until they were out of here and she was safe. Right now they shouldn't waste any energy on fighting.

"Is everyone all right?" he asked the women in Spanish. They had stayed in their cell, had kept down and kept quiet through the exchange of fire. "Sí, *señor*," a frightened voice said after a minute from the back. "We are okay."

"Don't come out yet," he warned, not that they looked as if they were ready for a rush to freedom. "It's not over yet, but soon. I promise."

He turned to Grace. "Stay here." He gave the order in his best I-mean-it voice, in case she was thinking about disobeying him again.

Then he carefully moved to the stairs, weapon ready. With the machines going in the wire mill, and them down below the ground, there was a chance that nobody had heard the shooting. He sure hoped and prayed that was the case. Because if someone *had* heard, then more attackers would be coming, and the backup he'd called for was still nowhere to be seen.

SHE KNEW SHE WAS NO LONGER the best. She knew she was washed-up, no longer fit for a military op. But the way Ryder had dismissed her still cut to the quick. Hurt her more than if it'd come from anyone else. Grace ground her teeth together and stood in silence, two dozen steps behind him.

He'd as much as said that she was nothing but a liability.

Fine. Whatever. But if things came to the worst, she'd still rather go out fighting than hiding behind others.

She couldn't see the top of the stairs from where she stood, so she watched Ryder for clues. No sign of weakness in *him*. His whole body was focused, his posture just right to launch into action at a moment's notice as he stood on the balls of his feet, gun aimed, eyes forward. He was a warrior through and through; nobody could doubt that looking at him.

As unbearably bossy and irritating as he was, everything about his warrior's body called out to her. Humiliating—considering how quickly he'd dismissed her. Annoying—considering that she didn't even like him. But her hormones didn't much care about that. They simply overrode her brain and sent her body all kinds of confusing signals.

Just great.

He tensed, giving a small nod that immediately redirected her thoughts.

She pulled her weapon up. Had he heard someone coming?

Despite the fact that she could have cheerfully strangled him more than once since they'd met, concern for him sliced through her.

He aimed. She stepped forward to back him up.

But he lowered his weapon the next moment, his muscles relaxing.

No more than two seconds passed when Shep came out of the staircase, as well armed as she'd ever seen him. "What do we have here?"

Mo followed him. "The building is secured."

"How?" Ryder asked.

"Immigration."

"Had to be called in," Shep added. "The mill is a large civilian, U.S. target. We couldn't just come in guns blaring."

He didn't sound happy. All three men looked pretty grim, in fact. Having to call in the INS was obviously an impediment to whatever secret mission they were working.

"Where are they?" she asked.

"Sealing the exits and checking ID's."

"Where are the captives?" Mo asked. "We have ambulances waiting outside, if they need medical help."

Grace tucked her weapon into her belt and walked to the cell, ducked inside. "You are safe," she told the women, and waited while the one who spoke English translated.

"Nobody is going to hurt you now. The bad guys are going to be caught. You can go home to your families."

But they cried and hung on to each other, not believing a word she was saying.

"Come, please."

For a while nobody moved. Then the tallest one took a few steps, set foot outside the cell at last. And little by little, seeing that nobody was harming them, at least not yet, the others followed.

Grace stifled a gasp when they came out into the light. Their rags were worse than she realized. Nearly all of them had bruises. One couldn't walk; the others had to support her. And, God, they were young. Somewhere between fourteen and nineteen—not women, but girls.

Ryder came up to them, slowly, his whole demeanor changed. He spoke in a low voice, gently in Spanish. If he'd looked like a warrior before, now he seemed a guardian angel, his gestures and words softened. He talked for a minute or two, ended the crying—mostly. Then he picked up the injured woman into his arms and carried her toward the stairs.

Mo and Shep came to support others. Grace did the same, although her ribs ached enough to make breathing difficult. But she knew that whatever abuse she'd endured from the bastards for the short time she'd been in captivity was nothing compared to what these girls had gone through in the past two months here.

Nobody spoke, the only sounds were feet shuffling, the machines humming somewhere in the mill and the quiet crying of one of the girls.

None of them could make it up the stairs on their own. Their muscles had little chance to move in that small cell for the past two months, and they were half-starved. Shep and Mo each supported two—one on each side—Ryder carried one while letting another lean on him. Grace held up the last one, although with the brace throwing off her balance, it wasn't always clear which one of them was holding up the other.

Conquering the stairs took forever.

Jamie and Keith rushed to help when the procession reached the top. Apparently, they'd been securing the hallway up there. She'd met all of Ryder's team now, several times when they were out on her land. Out of the six-man team, only Ray was missing, probably back at the office to coordinate things from there. He had a broken leg, his cast a lot more cumbersome than the brace she was wearing.

They exited the building at the back of the mill, among giant wire reels of copper, aluminum and steel. Not a single worker in sight.

"I guess when the INS says lockdown, they mean lockdown," Grace murmured to Ryder.

Several ambulances waited by the tractor trailers in the back. Due to a still-existing threat of violence, INS hadn't cleared the medics to enter the building, apparently. But they went to work the second the girls had been led to them. INS agents secured the area, hanging back for now, letting the ambulance crew do their job.

The young women couldn't open their eyes in the bright sunlight and were quickly helped into the back of the ambulances. The medics, half of them Hispanic, started IVs, all friendly and smiling, speaking to them in Spanish to reassure them while their injuries were checked.

Ryder's team rushed back into the building, but he remained at her side. "When the medics are done with the girls, I want them to look you over."

"I want world peace." She moved away from him, ready to go home and take a shower, then remembered that he was her ride.

She hated to ask a favor of him, but she did it, anyway. "I'd really like to leave. Do you think I could borrow your SUV?" She'd had pretty much all she could handle for one day, and he had all his buddies here. Catching a ride wouldn't be an issue for him.

He watched her for a wordless second, dropped the keys into her palm, then held out his hand. "I want the gun."

Of course. It was evidence. She handed the weapon over. He tucked it behind his back, next to his own, then lifted a hand to her face and rubbed his thumb over her chin.

"You've got a few smudges here."

Her nerve endings came to life.

"The thought that those bastards touched you is killing me," he said.

"Not to worry. I didn't go down easy."

He gave a reluctant, dimpled smile.

He stood too close and the air got sucked out of that small space between them all of a sudden. She couldn't move back, just kept staring at him. His desert-honey eyes watched her and his gaze softened. For a second, his thumb brushed against the edge of her lip, and desire leaped to life inside her, sharp and insistent, stealing her breath.

"Grace." Her name was a whisper on his lips.

"Yo! Are you coming, man?" Mo shouted through one of the upstairs windows.

Ryder dropped his hands. "I need to talk to you later," he told her, "when I'm done here."

Since she couldn't form words, she feebly nodded, then turned her back and walked away from him.

She didn't stop until she was at his SUV. She got in, then leaned her forehead against the steering wheel. The car smelled like him: man and gun oil and a faint trace of aftershave.

She wanted *not* to like it, but she did.

God, she really did need some time away from him. She'd been getting under his spell somehow, little by little. She wanted a break.

Later, she would call him to find out what happened with the girls, to make sure they were taken care of and to offer to help if she could. They could talk, although, she was afraid it'd be all just him yelling at her for getting into so much trouble. But for now, she needed to get out of here.

She drove out of town, her mind a jumble of images. And by the time she reached the quiet country roads, she realized that while she needed time away from Ryder, she didn't want to be alone. So she took the turnoff toward Dylan's ranch. Girlfriend time.

The Rogers place was well kept, new roof, a row of yellow roses trimming the wraparound porch that held a half-dozen rockers. Comparing it to the abandoned-looking Cordero ranch made her a little sad. Maybe she could stay an extra few days, hire a couple of guys and work on the house a little.

Not that she changed her mind about not wanting to stay. But if she ended up selling, the place would bring a better price if it didn't look ready to collapse. Dylan wanted only the land. Maybe she could sell the house with a couple of acres separately.

"Gracie!" Molly ran out the front door as soon as Grace parked in the driveway, followed by three excited dogs. "Is that a new car? I didn't recognize it. How have you been?" As she got closer, she slowed, her eyes going wide. "Oh, my Lord… Are you all right? What happened? Your ankle, I know about, but…were you in an accident?" She glanced with confusion at the car, which was spotless, then back at her.

"I'm fine." Grace dusted herself off, a little self-conscious suddenly.

She supposed she did have a few new scratches and bruises, and her clothes did show signs of her being rolled around in that basement. She wasn't sure how much she could say, considering that Ryder was working on a top secret mission. But word of what happened at the mill would get out. The workers would be talking about immigration officials descending.

"INS raided the mill," she said.

"How on earth did you get caught up in that? Never mind that now. Let's get you off your feet. Come in, come in." Molly linked arms with her and dragged her toward the house. "You look like you've been through a stampede. Let me fix you up a little."

That little fix-up, as it turned out, meant a scented hot bath, every scratch disinfected and bandaged, clean clothes, and a hot meal of burritos and a cold marga-rita. But by the end, Grace did feel considerably more human.

"I missed you," Molly said when she stopped fuss-ing and they were sitting at the kitchen table.

"I missed you, too. How is Logan?" she asked at last. Molly had gotten pregnant right out of high school. She'd never told anyone who the father was, not even her best friend, but had been adamant about keeping the baby.

"In school. He's smart as a tick, that kid." She grinned. "You wouldn't believe how big he is. And thank God for that. We've had issues." She rolled her eyes.

"Such as?"

"That know-it-all Missy Nasher's kid calling Logan a bastard in class." Some red crept onto her face. "I put up with her and her phony friends calling me, well, whatever they called me all those years after I got preg-nant. But I swear, she's not going to start in on Logan. I'm about ready to go down to the shop and have a talk with her. I'm only cooling it because Logan begged."

"There are things I love about small towns, and there I things I hate about small towns," Grace said. "People just need to get over themselves."

"Most of them are fine folks. The rest of them can go to hell," Molly said with a lot of feeling.

Grace nodded. "I hope I'll get to see that boy one of these days. I'll come back again. And thank you for breakfast this morning," she added, remembering sud-denly. Morning seemed years away.

Molly gave a little wave. "Don't even mention it. Now tell me how you came to be at the mill. I mean how insane is that? You go about your business and get caught up in something like this. The world just gets weirder and weirder."

"I went there to talk to Bobbi about Tommy's dirt bike. Ended up right in the middle of the roundup."

Molly's expression turned fierce as she reached for her cell phone. "You know what? I'm going to give Shane a piece of my mind about that."

"Had nothing to do with the sheriff. He wasn't even there. It was all INS."

She set the phone down with a disgusted look on her face. "You should file an official complaint."

"I came here for a few days of peace."

"You brought Tommy back." Her face saddened. "You must feel so alone without him. He was something, wasn't he?"

They shared a smile.

"What would I have to do for you to take pity on my clueless brother and marry him?" Molly asked after a minute.

"He's a successful businessman. He's hardly clueless."

Molly shrugged. "It's all about the money these days. I barely see him. All he does is work. When he's not out hunting with those new shady-looking buddies of his. Not on your land," she added quickly.

Around here, pretty much everyone knew about Grace's safe haven agreement and people respected it.

"What shady-looking buddies?"

"Outsiders. From West Texas, I guess." Her tone added a wealth of meaning to her words. "Too many people moving in. What do people have to move for, anyway? They should just all stay where they're at."

Grace grinned. Molly had always hated change. She hadn't moved a chair since Grace had been here the last time. She kept the house spotlessly clean, but she hadn't updated much in the past couple of years.

"Do you ever get lonely out here?" Dylan had his apartment in Hullett, and Grace suspected he stayed there a fair share of his time.

"I've got Logan and the dogs. Hogs and horses, too," Molly said, then straightened suddenly. "Speaking of which, Skipper has a bad back. I thought maybe you could look at him in a few days when your ankle felt better. I was going to call you about that."

"Now is as good time as any." Grace looked around for the dog, but they seemed to have all gone outside. "One of your margaritas and I feel no pain. You always had a heavy hand with the liquor," she said as a private joke. In fact, Molly rarely drank. But back when she'd gotten pregnant with Logan, some of the mean girls had started a rumor about her and drinking.

Molly just laughed at her. "That's why I have so many guests."

"Brings in the gentleman callers, does it?"

"Don't believe the gossip." She gave another laugh. "If everything they said about me in Hullett was true, I'd have blisters."

Grace winced. "O-kay. How about that dog, then?"

Since she had a drink, she was going to hang around for a while, anyway. She didn't drink and drive, as a rule, not even on slow country roads with no traffic.

The three dogs ran up to them the second the back door opened. Molly patted and hugged them with the same outpouring of love that she did everything. It was a shame that someone like her would be alone, Grace thought, and wondered if she might end up like this someday, all alone. Except, she wouldn't even have the ranch—if she sold it to Dylan—and children to visit her when she got old, like Molly had Logan.

The thought grew into a hard rock inside her chest. And for some reason made her think of Ryder.

Chapter Ten

Ryder paced the porch in front of her door. The only thing keeping him from breaking through that door was that he knew Grace wasn't inside. His SUV wasn't in the driveway.

He'd borrowed Jamie's car to come here to make sure she was all right, and couldn't find her anywhere. She wasn't answering her cell phone, either. Maybe she hadn't retrieved it in all the chaos. He planned on staying until she returned. Jamie shouldn't need the car for a while; he was the operations coordinator and had plenty of computer work at the office.

The man was supposed to work mostly at the office, anyway. He'd lost both legs overseas on a mission. He'd left the SDDU for a while before the Colonel had brought him back on the team. He'd been in a wheelchair at the time, brought in for office work specifically. He'd gotten some fancy prosthetic limbs since, however, and now you couldn't keep him from the field for anything.

Since they had no official team leader for this location yet, there was no one to tell him differently. Although, Ryder was pretty sure even a team leader couldn't do much to rein Jamie Cassidy in.

Truth was, the team thing was still strange for all of them. They were used to being overseas, deep undercover, doing lone wolf operations that involved intelligence gathering, search and rescue and the odd assassination. But the current situation called for a different setup. And whatever the country needed, they were ready to do it.

He watched the road for Grace. He shouldn't have let her leave the mill by herself, dammit.

By the time his SUV rumbled up the long driveway with Grace behind the wheel, the tires kicking up a cloud of dust, he worked himself into a fine state. He strode toward her. She'd been missing for close to two hours. Where in hell had she been?

Not that she had the good sense to look contrite.

She actually looked surprised to see him there. As if she'd expected him to just go about his job without checking to make sure that she was okay.

She was a major pain. An aggravation of epic proportions. Had a thorough dislike of authority. Never did what she was told.

He pitied the man who was someday going to marry her.

"What's wrong with you?" she asked as he got closer. "You've got that bossy, constipated look on your face. Like you're about to start handing out orders, or deliver some military discipline."

What's wrong with *him?* "You didn't come straight home."

"I went to see a friend. No need to get your boxer shorts into a bunch."

How the hell did she know he wore boxer shorts?

Okay, right, she'd cut his pants off him the night

she'd saved him. Part of him wished he'd been awake for that. A completely inappropriate reaction. And further proof of just how much she messed up his head.

"Things can't go on like this, Grace. You are going to pull back. You are not going to put yourself into harm's way again. Do you hear me?"

Her face got all pinched for a second, then her lips narrowed and her eyes blazed with fury. "Because I'm damaged goods? Because I'm not as strong as you are physically and mentally?" Her voice rose.

"There are all kinds of strengths, Grace. You are—"

"Don't you try to placate me. I know what you think when you look at me, that I'm a crazy freaking cripple!"

He stared at her for a second. "That's not what I think when I look at you. Believe me."

He stepped up to her, real close, got right in her face. Then he put his hands on her shoulders, pulled her even closer and crushed his lips against hers.

Ninety-nine percent of him needed a taste of her with a desperation that bordered on insanity. The one percent that could still think expected her to hit him over the head with something. But even the threat of pain couldn't stop him.

He moved his lips over hers, angled his head for better access, gentled his hands on her and slipped them off her shoulders so his arms could go completely around her.

He tasted her bottom lip, then the top one, breathed in her fresh scent of soap, but didn't spend much time wondering how she'd met up with a bath on her way home. The feel of her in his arms was too intoxicating to ponder anything else except how to get closer.

The full length of her body pressed against his felt

like a miracle. He licked the seam of her lips, and when she yielded, his tongue swept inside, his throat releasing a primal groan that was so full of need it bordered on embarrassing.

He wanted her. All the way. Now.

On the hood of his SUV.

He backed her that way, lifted her, feeling damned gratified when her legs wrapped around his waist, her soft core coming into contact with his hardness that strained for her.

This was so right. So *right*.

Except… She was the wrong woman.

Not that the hormone surge that took over his brain gave a damn. She tasted like strawberries, and a very faint taste of good tequila.

He went on kissing her for another long minute.

Then, with great reluctance, he pulled away.

Her clear, emerald eyes had gone all soft. He stepped away from her all the way before he could go back for seconds like he wanted.

She slipped off the hood of his car and stared at him, frozen to the spot where she stood.

He summoned up whatever self-control he had and restarted his brain. "Where were you?" He'd be damned if he apologized for this kiss.

"At the Rogerses' ranch."

Exactly the wrong thing to say. Dylan freaking Rogers. He took two steps forward, reached for her and pulled her to him again. Was ready to claim her as his…

Then caught that sheer insanity at the last split second.

I shouldn't be doing this.

But he couldn't let go just yet, either. So he leaned his

forehead against hers, hoping some great outside power, like say an earthquake, would somehow pull him away.

She didn't punch him in the chin as she should have. She closed her eyes instead.

Which was all the encouragement he needed.

He kissed her gently this time, taking his time, savoring the moment. *There. Nice and easy.* He'd overreacted before. A simple kiss didn't have to be unmanageable. Then he deepened the kiss and lost control all over again.

Chemistry hit him like a daisy cutter—the bunker-busting bombs the military used these days. *No escape.*

Possibly hours passed before the first thread of common sense returned. She was hurt. He was practically engaged. Well, as soon as he found the right woman. He needed to stop this.

But her lips felt too good under his; her taste intoxicated him. *Okay. The end. Step away from temptation.*

"Don't do this," he said in a raspy whisper as he pulled away.

Her heavy-lidded eyes cleared, then rounded, her eyebrows sliding up her forehead. Her hands moved up to her hips. "What do you mean don't do this? *I* didn't attack you in the middle of the driveway." Color rose in her cheeks.

He tried to untangle his thoughts, but didn't quite succeed. "I was talking to myself. I'm getting married."

Shock crossed her face. Then she kicked him in the shin, hard, before she marched away.

"Grace," he called after her. "It's not like that. Let me explain." He went after her.

She slowed for a second, which gave him hope, but she only reached into her pockets for his car keys and flung them at his head. Then she marched right into her house and slammed the door in his face.

"I was just trying to be honest," he shouted after her as a radio came on inside, full blast, an upbeat country song about a woman walking all over men in her cowboy boots.

He tried again. "What I meant was that as much as I like you, I'm not available that way."

No response came. She probably didn't hear a word he said.

He licked the taste of her from his bottom lip, registered again the definite trace of tequila and strawberries, her flowery soap scent still in his nose. She'd had a bath and a drink at the Rogerses' ranch.

The urge to break down the door and demand an explanation was overpowering. Not that he was a jealous man. Not once, ever before.

He ran his fingers through his hair. She had him turned inside out so badly, he had no idea anymore what kind of man he was, or what he really wanted.

He turned on his heels and strode to his car, shouting out over his shoulders as he went. "I will be back. We will talk. This is not over. And stay away from Dylan Rogers!"

The music stopped; a window flew open. "I was visiting with his sister, Molly!" The window slammed shot, and the music went back to blaring.

SHE JUST HAD THE BEST KISS of her life and it had come from the most infuriating man God had ever created. Who was apparently engaged. As if the other hundred reasons they were all wrong for each other weren't enough.

Engaged. That thought hurt so much it stole her breath.

Grace stood behind the curtained window and watched him drive away, his tires kicking up a dust storm. She turned the radio off, before her ears could suffer permanent damage. And then just stood there, confused and furious, going over all that had just happened and unable to make any sense of it.

When the sound of a car's motor from outside reached her, she was ready to go for Gramps's rifle, but then she recognized the familiar rumbling and moved to the window unarmed. Jamie was driving her pickup. She'd left it at the ravine the night before.

He didn't come to the door, and she didn't go outside. She simply watched as he walked with an uneven gate to the SUV Ryder had left here, since he took his own car when he'd stormed away.

She liked Jamie, although he was probably the most closed-off guy on the team. From what she'd caught from the others when she'd been out showing them her land, she pieced together that he'd lost his legs in the military and had been in a wheelchair until recently. He was some sort of a legend. The others clearly respected him a great deal. Now he was walking again with the help of his space tech prostheses. Not that he ever talked about any of that.

She would have to thank him for bringing her pickup back, thank them all for the rescue at the mill. And she would, the next time she saw them. But not today. God, she needed a little breather. It'd been a hell of a day.

She was fed and bathed, which left her little to do for the rest of the afternoon but clean up the house a little and take care of the horses. Later, when the urge to strangle Ryder more or less passed, she would call him and ask whether his team had turned up any new information at the train station. They were probably out there right now, interviewing people.

She needed to give them time to do their job. Which left a couple of empty hours. She walked Cookie then did laundry. Cleaned up the kitchen. Her gaze found the urn on the mantel. She still hadn't done what she'd come here for. She'd been procrastinating and she knew it.

"God, I wish you were still here. Everything is turning into such a mess, Tommy."

Her heart constricted. She wasn't ready to say a final goodbye to her brother, not yet. And she wasn't sure if she would ever be fully ready.

"Hey, there, Twinky," she told the cat who finally slinked forward from one of her hiding places. The two hundred decibels of country rock had been a little too much for her. The kittens immediately charged at her and showered her with affection, and the cat shot Grace a pained look.

"Get used to it, buddy. They think you're their surrogate mother. It won't be that bad. It's actually pretty nice to have family."

Her mind was full of images of her brother. Them riding together, him protecting her at school. She'd sneaked out a few times in the night to meet up with friends for some wild ATV rides. He'd followed to make sure she wouldn't get hurt. Man, that had made her mad at the time.

She hadn't wanted him to treat her like a little sister. She'd been in such a rush to be a grown-up. So she'd decided to give him a taste of his own medicine, and had followed him the next time he did the sneaking.

He was meeting big-boobs Sally at the old feed store. Of course, he'd caught Grace and had nearly wrung her neck. Didn't buy the story that she was only there to protect him.

The memory put a smile on her face.

She would have never gotten caught if she hadn't tripped over the old railroad tracks in the dark and made a ruckus.

Her smile froze.

The old feed store had been a train station back in the day, maybe fifty or so years ago. It stood right on the west border of the ranch.

An abandoned old train station.

Out in the boondocks. That made more sense than hiding illegals at the bustling station at Edinburg. If Miguel and Rosita had been last seen at a train station, Grace was willing to bet good money that this was it.

She reached for her phone, but it wasn't in her pocket. In the chaos, she'd left it at the mill, had forgotten to take it back from the bastard who'd grabbed it from her before he'd beaten her. The landline to the ranch had been long disconnected. She couldn't afford paying for something like that when nobody was using it.

Nightfall was still at least an hour away. She could just drive out there, take a look, see if she had anything to report. She wasn't looking forward to talking with Ryder. If she didn't absolutely have to call him, she'd just as soon avoid it.

But going out there alone didn't seem like the smartest thing to do.

Dylan, she thought. The Rogers ranch was one of the closest to her, and there was a fifty-fifty chance that Dylan would be showing up right about now for dinner.

And even if he wasn't there, she could tell Molly about the station, so somebody would know where she'd gone, in case something bad happened to her.

She stepped into her boots and went outside. Better check on Cookie one more time before she left. The horses snorted a greeting as she opened the barn door and they recognized her.

"You two having fun in here?" Now where was that damn bucket again?

She spotted it in the corner where she could have sworn she didn't leave it.

Then she froze as puzzle pieces fell into place.

The barn door that kept opening. The bucket that kept moving. The strange noises that came from the barn some nights.

She moved to the door, switched on every single light switch and grabbed the pitchfork. And then she moved forward to investigate.

The ladder to the hayloft creaked under her boots as she put her weight on it. "If anyone is up there, show yourself now," she demanded.

But no sounds came from up above. The horses didn't act skittish, either. They were looking at her curiously.

She moved up rung by rung, her muscles tightening. But she found no one up there. The hayloft was empty, covered in dust and cobwebs.

She relaxed as she climbed back down. "I think I'm becoming paranoid."

But she decided to check the back of the barn, anyway, for signs that someone might have been in here at one point. The stalls were all either empty or filled with miscellaneous equipment. An antique hoe sat in the back corner of the barn. Everything back there had been there since before Tommy had to leave.

Except the hay.

She stared at the fresh pile on the ground.

For what? She sure as anything hadn't put it there.

She thrust the pitchfork into it and moved it around, found the trapdoor in less than a minute.

Now *that* definitely hadn't been there before.

She wedged the prongs of the pitchfork into the gap and heaved, springing the door open. She stared down into the darkness, the space barely lit by the light that hung from a beam above her.

The bolt hole was maybe four feet high, but fairly big. Ten feet by ten feet, at least. It was reinforced with four-by-fours just like the tunnel in the ravine had been.

A temporary holding place, she guessed, pretty sure it was connected to the smuggling.

A phone would have been nice right about now.

She closed the door, shuffled the hay around on top of it until everything looked like it had when she'd come back here.

"What do you two know about this?" she asked the horses once she walked back to them.

They ignored her. They were more interested in their feed.

She made sure they had everything they needed. She turned back from the door on her way out. "You two better keep an eye on the place."

She'd tell Ryder about this when she called him about the feed store.

Once inside the house, she grabbed a flashlight. The old feed store was boarded up and would be dark inside.

She grabbed her grandfather's rifle, too. And hoped like anything that she wouldn't have to use it.

She drove straight to the Rogerses' ranch, felt a burst of optimism when she saw Dylan's fancy new truck in the driveway. It was the only car there. Maybe Molly had to run to town for something.

But it was Molly and the dogs, once again, that ran down the driveway to meet her.

"Hey, I was just about to run to Hullett to pick up Logan. He's at his karate lesson," she said. "Want to come with me?"

"Can't right now. Is Dylan here?"

"Off hog hunting with his buddies." She rolled her eyes. "He traded cars with me. Didn't want his fancy one to get dirty."

"Mind if I call him on your phone? I lost mine today."

"Sure." Molly dialed the number then handed the phone over. "Is everything okay?"

The other end rang over and over, then switched to voice mail. "Hi, Dylan. It's Grace. Could you meet me at the old feed store? I'm heading over there right now. I hope you get this." She handed the phone back.

Molly watched her. "Are you in some kind of trouble?"

She shook her head. "This has to do with the smuggling. I think the bastards who built the tunnel might be keeping some of the people who come over at the old feed store."

"That's dangerous stuff, Gracie. Should you be getting involved with this? Why not just call Shane? He'd come right out with his deputies."

"It's just a hunch. I'm just going to drive over there. See what's going on. If there's anything, I'll call the law. I promise. I don't suppose you have an extra cell phone in the house?"

"Here." Molly handed over her own. "You take this."

"Thanks. I'll be back with it in a couple of hours." She tucked the phone in her pocket and ran her fingers through her hair. "I'm probably just paranoid." She shrugged. "Sometimes… I spent so much time looking over my shoulder, always watching for danger, for roadside explosives and snipers and all that stuff. It's hard to learn to relax again. I still tend to see danger in everything."

"There's plenty of danger out there. Better to be safe than sorry. Want me to come with you?"

"No way. There's not going to be any trouble. I promise. Even if worse comes to worst, I have practice at this. And Dylan is coming to meet me. You go get Logan."

But Molly still didn't look sure. "Do you want one of Dylan's hunting rifles? He only took the big one."

"I got Gramps's. Not that I'm planning on using it."

THE DRIVE WAS LONG, HOT AND DUSTY. Then she ran out of pavement and hit gravel, which was worse yet. She got all bounced around by the time she reached her target.

And immediately realized that coming alone had been a mistake.

Two pickups stood behind the old feed store that had started its life as a train station. The place wasn't nearly as abandoned as everyone believed. Which didn't mean that anything nefarious was going on here—she tried for optimism. Could be someone bought the old place to start a new business.

She pulled her truck behind a couple of large boulders, got out and crept to the edge of the first one, checked the area for snakes and other nasty stuff, then lay down on her stomach.

She took Molly's phone out and switched it to vibrate in case Dylan called her back. She thought about calling Ryder. Okay, it really was stupid to be out here alone. She dialed and waited until Ryder answered. "I'm out at the old feed store on Rowley Road."

Two men came from the building as she said that. Each led a small child by the hand.

"Rosita and Miguel are here," she whispered, even though they were way too far to hear her. She definitely recognized the kids from the picture.

Her heart lurched, and a hard knot deep inside her relaxed. She'd hoped and prayed that the children were still alive, but a part of her knew all along there was a chance that they weren't. Seeing them brought relief, even if she was far from being able to rescue them.

"Stay where you are. I'm on my way," Ryder told her. "How bad is it?"

Two more men came from the building.

"Four armed men that I can see."

"You're not to engage them in any way. Do you hear me?"

"I'm not stupid."

"No, you're not. You just think nothing of your own life when there's someone else to save. Grace? Please."

Was tough guy Ryder McKay begging? "I'm flat on the ground, two hundred yards back from the place, okay?"

"Stay there. I mean it."

She heard a door slam on the other end of the line and a motor start. He was in his SUV.

The men she watched piled into the pickups with the kids.

"They're leaving."

"I don't want you to follow. We'll follow the tracks when I get there."

It would be dark by then. And every wasted minute gave those bastards a chance to hand the kids over to someone else. No way would she let them slip through her fingers. "Sorry."

"Grace, listen to me—"

She hung up on him and got back into her truck, her phone vibrating in her pocket. She ignored it. She didn't want to argue with Ryder right now. She needed to focus on those kids.

Chapter Eleven

Ryder gave up on reaching Grace and called the rest of his team instead, although they were pretty far away, checking leads at the train station in Edinburg.

"Grace found the Molinero kids. She's out on Rowley Road. I'm on my way."

"We're leaving right now," Mo told him. "Got exact coordinates?"

"I wish. She's at some old feed store."

"Don't worry about it. We'll find the place."

He had no doubt of that. The question was, would they find it in time, or would they be too late?

He tore down the road, following the GPS directions. Finding Rowley Road wouldn't be an issue. Finding a feed store that had been out of business probably from before GPS was invented was another matter. Especially when Rowley Road was over a hundred miles long.

His fingers gripped the wheel hard. He headed toward the section of the road that stretched between Hullett and the Cordero ranch, figuring it to be his best bet.

He called back the number she'd called him from. She didn't pick up.

Was she ignoring him, or was she hurt? "Dammit, Grace."

Fear like he'd never experienced before punched through him instead of the usual adrenaline that came when an op suddenly turned interesting. Fear wasn't good. It didn't help in the least.

He was a soldier. He was in control. At all times.

Except around Grace.

THE MEN WHO HAD THE KIDS took a dirt road that crossed her land, and fury bubbled up in Grace. This was her ranch, not some criminal playground. What made people think that they had free rein on someone else's property?

She was probably to blame at least partially— absentee ownership. She'd been away too much for too long. Tommy had been here before he'd gotten truly sick, but he hadn't been well enough for a long time by that point to regularly ride or drive over the whole ranch. And now Dylan, although he rented, wasn't exactly a full-timer out here, either. He lived elsewhere; he had other businesses.

She followed the trucks for a couple of miles. The dirt road they drove didn't really go anywhere in particular, just meandered among the pastures. It'd been marked out back when her grandfather still had a thriving horse ranch.

She could only think of one building out this way, a log cabin nobody had used in ages, originally built back in the eighteen hundreds by one of her ancestors. She was fairly sure the men were heading there so she could afford to hang back enough not to be noticed.

She stopped her car a quarter mile away, pulled it way off the road into the brush, then hobbled the rest of the way, as fast as she could with her brace. When she was close enough to see the building, she kept down, moving from cover to cover.

Since dusk was falling, she hoped she wouldn't be seen. The cabin had few windows, and those small but numerous gaps between the logs that hadn't been re-chinked in decades.

She pulled the phone, saw the dozen missed calls from Ryder, and sent a text. Take dirt rd south to old cabin. Then she turned the phone off. Once she reached the building, even a low buzzing could give her away.

A couple of camping lanterns lit up the derelict build-ing. She rounded it silently and noted the two trucks up front, the ones she'd followed here. The sound of an approaching vehicle reached her from the distance. Someone else was coming.

She crept up to the window and peered in, keeping low. She could only see the kids, crying, and the four men she'd seen at the station, nobody new. She moved into the deepest shadows and she waited.

Dylan's old pickup pulled up.

He shouldn't be here, she thought in near panic. He had no idea what he was walking into. Keeping low, she rushed forward toward him as he got out.

He looked pretty startled to see her.

"What are you doing here?" she whispered.

"I was just driving around. Saw cars at the cabin. Figured I'd see who they were."

"Smugglers. With guns. I tried to call you."

He glanced toward the cabin, but didn't duck down like she had.

The men inside had to have heard his truck. They'd be coming in a second to investigate. "Dylan," she whis-pered his name, trying to tug him down, into cover.

But he just looked at her. "Why don't you go home? I'll deal with this."

Her instincts prickled.

She didn't like this setup. She didn't want to think that he could be involved. Not in something like this, dammit. But as she turned to step back from him, she caught sight of the front of his old pickup. Now that the headlights were turned off, she could see the front better.

She stared at the spot where the Chevy emblem should have been.

Last time she'd seen the truck he'd given to his sister when he bought his brand-new one, Molly had it parked toward the garage, so Grace hadn't seen that end.

She tore her gaze from the vehicle, fighting to keep her face impassive as the little hairs stood up on the back of her neck. "Good idea. My foot is killing me, anyway. I hate this damn brace. I'm supposed to go to dinner to Maddie's. I'm already running late." She brought up the sheriff's wife, insinuating that if she were late, Shane would be looking for her.

She calculated how long it would take her to get the rifle off her shoulder. Too long. He'd tackle her at the first sign of her trying to make a move. And they were too close to each other for the weapon to be of much use, anyway. She began to move around him, exaggerating her limp, and was almost clear when he grabbed her.

"I can see you thinking." He pulled a handgun from behind his back with his free hand. "You're too damn smart, you know that? Wish you were the type to walk away from trouble, but you never do," he said with regret. "I'm sorry, Gracie."

"Don't do this, Dylan." She did go for the rifle then.

But he had the advantage, since he was already holding her other arm, and he stood steadier on his feet than she did at the moment. He knocked her against the logs and yanked the rifle away from her. "You shouldn't have come here. Pull your phone from your pocket and toss it."

She did as she was told. She'd already texted Ryder where she was going. The phone had done its job. It wasn't worth getting shot over.

Not that she could even comprehend the fact that Dylan shooting her was an issue here. The sense of betrayal that swept through her threatened to drown her. "You're better than this."

"It's too tough to make a living from ranching anymore."

"But you have the survival training."

"That don't bring in nearly enough. We had a good run for a while, but now… Corporations are cutting back on all nonessential spending. Team-building vacations go first."

"You have other businesses. How much stupid money do you need?"

He shrugged. "The dealership is about ready to go under. People hang on to their cars longer in a recession. Then there's Molly and Logan."

Okay, so fine, he helped out his sister and his nephew. She knew that. "But smuggling? Kidnapping kids? Are you kidding me? You know Molly would rather eat dirt than take money that came from something like this."

He had the decency to look uncomfortable. "It's not what it looks like. The kids are orphans."

"You have a nephew, dammit. Think of him. What would Molly say?"

His face and his hold on her tightened. "Leave my family out of this." Then he made a visible effort to relax. "These kids will be fine. I promise. Look, the parents sneaked them over the border. The adults didn't make it—the kids did. Would you want them to be returned to poverty? They'll have a better life here. I'm doing this to help everyone, Gracie."

Except he wasn't. Everything he said was a lie and he knew it. Paco had died with that Chevy emblem in his fist. Which meant Dylan had been there when Paco had been killed. Her brain could just barely process that.

She scanned the area for an avenue of escape, and came up empty. Dylan had both guns. No way could he afford to let her go at this stage. But since she had nothing to lose, she decided to try, anyway.

"Just drive away with your friends. I'll take the children to the authorities. I'll tell everyone that I found them wandering on my land. They're too young. They have no idea what's going on. They could never identify you. This could still turn out okay for everyone here."

But he shook his head. "We both know you're not the type to let something like this go, Gracie."

"Maybe we don't know each other as well as we thought we did. I thought you were different. Never in a million years could I have conceived that you'd do something like this. I'm standing here, and I still can't believe it."

He gave a sour laugh. "You thought I was what? Like your sainted brother? He risked his life for his country, never did anything wrong in his whole life, and look where it got him."

He started out toward the house and dragged her with him. "I didn't want you to be involved, I swear. You should have spread Tommy's ashes then gone home. These kids would have been just fine without you. They'll have all that good American life their parents dreamed up for them."

"They have a mother. Her name is Esperanza and she's worried to death. She would do anything to get them back."

"She'll have more brats. Those people have them by the bushel."

"*Those people?* Seriously? Do you even hear the way you're talking? Don't do this, Dylan."

He wouldn't look at her. "The stakes are too high. It's not the kind of business a person can get involved in then walk away when they no longer like it. I couldn't walk away if I wanted to, Gracie." His jaw tightened. "It's not my fault that you put yourself in the middle of this."

Then they reached the door and he shoved her inside, letting her go at last.

Four men looked at her with surprise on their swarthy faces. The children huddled in the far corner, looking scared.

If she was the sole captive, she would have chosen that moment to make her last stand, gone for one of their weapons and tried to take out as many of them as possible. But initiating a gunfight was out of the question with the children in the room, so she remained passive for the time being, waiting for a better opportunity.

"Tie her up," Dylan ordered the men, who got moving rapidly.

"Hey!" he yelled at the one who grabbed her too hard, as if on reflex. Then he caught himself, and turned away from her, walked outside.

They tied her hands then shoved her—a little less roughly—to the corner where the kids were sitting on a horse blanket. One of the men pushed her down next to the children with a stupid smirk on his face.

She flashed the twins an encouraging smile as she looked them over. They were frightened and dirty, but didn't appear starved or hurt. "It's okay," she whispered, not sure how much English they understood. So she added, *"Bueno. Todos Buenos,"* before turning to Dylan, who was coming back in, carrying a duffel bag.

"We can still fix this."

He held her gaze in the dim cabin for a few seconds before he shook his head. "No, we can't." He tossed her the duffel bag. "Clean them up and get them dressed."

She rifled through the contents awkwardly with her tied-up hands, hoping for something she could use as a weapon, but found nothing save wet wipes, a comb and clean clothes for each child. The shorts and tops were nothing fancy, straight off the sales rack at Walmart.

"I could do this easier if my hands weren't tied."

Dylan turned back from the far corner where he was talking rapidly under his breath with the men. "You'll manage." He turned his back to her again.

She glanced at the door. Sure, she could run. But he would catch up with her long before she reached her pickup. And even if, by some miracle, he didn't, bottom line was—no way could she leave the children behind now that she'd found them.

Rosita was hiding behind Miguel.

Grace held up the clothes to the boy and reached for him first. "It's okay. *Bueno.*"

He hesitated, but apparently understood enough to

know that neither of them had a choice, so after a few seconds he moved toward Grace.

She used a wet wipe to clean the boy's hands, then his face, which he resisted, but was too scared to completely pull away. *"Bueno,"* she said again, then helped him out of his clothes, yanked the tags off the new outfit and helped him put it on.

Since Rosita saw that nothing bad had happened to her brother, she let Grace clean and dress her without much fuss. Seeing the kids scared plain stiff was just too sad, kindling new anger inside Grace.

She made a point to give the little girl a big smile. *"Muy bonita."*

Rosita threw herself into her arms, and she held the child as best as she could with her hands tied. When the little girl pulled away, Grace flashed her another reassuring smile and picked up the comb. "We're going to fix your hair, all right? I promise to make it pretty."

Undoing the messed-up braid, combing all that hair and rebraiding it would have been a lot easier if her hands weren't bound. But she did manage a semidecent job.

Miguel took the comb on his own and fixed himself.

Dylan strode over. *"Vamos."* He barked the single word at the kids and reached for them.

They scampered behind Grace.

To hell with finding a weapon, her body was a weapon. She lurched to her feet and blocked Dylan. "No."

He shoved her aside.

She kicked at him, swaying precariously on her feet.

"Dammit, Grace." He jerked his head at the others,

who rushed over and grabbed her, dragging her out of the way.

She swore at Dylan, but he ignored her as he reached for the crying kids, who did their best to twist their hands out of his. Miguel even bit him.

Dylan shook the kid. "Enough," he thundered, then dragged them outside.

Grace fought with everything she had, not letting her aches and bruises stop her. "Dylan!" She lost her balance and ended up on the horse blanket, under the men.

The pickup's motor roared to life outside.

She pressed her fists together and brought them up as one, smacked one of the men holding her, snapping his head back hard enough so that he rolled off her.

The next one got a well-aimed kick between his legs, her knee jamming up hard into his most sensitive parts. He went white as he groaned, his hands falling away from her.

She struggled to stand, but only made it to her knees when another one came for her. "Dylan!"

Gravel crunched under tires as the pickup pulled away.

The last of the four men joined the fray, and between him and his buddy they knocked her on her back again. She wasn't sure whether they wanted simply to sub-.due her or something a lot worse, but she wasn't about to stop fighting so she could find out. She kicked, bit, scratched, using every bit of training she'd learned in the army, calling on every instinct she had.

A fast hook to her jaw left her seeing stars. She tasted blood. And the two men she'd temporarily disabled were reviving. *Oh, God.* She gritted her teeth. She didn't want to die here. Not like this.

She cast a desperate glance at the ground around her, looking for something to defend herself with. Nothing but the comb and the empty duffel bag.

She surged up, was knocked down again.

Then the door banged open and Dylan stood there, his eyes flashing with some dark emotion. *"Alto!"* he yelled at the men and brought up his gun. He hesitated before he shot the first one, but with the others after that, he didn't even blink.

Shock sliced through her as she stared at him, wiping blood off her face. Knowing he'd turned villain was one thing. Seeing him shoot people like that, even if in her defense, was...mind-boggling.

"Thank you." She desperately wanted to build some sort of connection so she hid her revulsion. "I knew you wouldn't go through with this. We have to take those kids to safety. I can help."

But he strode to her without his dark expression softening and yanked her to her feet.

"You and I, we've been through things, right?" She was mad at him, but incredibly sad, too, grieving for the man she'd believed him to be. He'd been one of the good guys once. A good friend. Molly's brother. *Oh, God.*

He didn't say anything.

He didn't have to. Didn't have to drag her after him, either. She followed him because she wanted to be with the kids.

She got into the pickup on her own. The children immediately burrowed against her, scared and quiet. Dylan stepped on the gas and drove into the darkness.

"Where are we going?"

He pressed his lips into a thin, angry line.

Fear sliced through her as she suddenly understood.

They weren't going anywhere. He meant to take care of her somewhere along the way. She'd seen too much. No way he could let her live. He hadn't decided to save her. He was simply giving her an easier death.

A shot to the head and a shove out the door, most likely.

She felt the shakes coming on as that image bounced around in her head. But she fought the darkness back. She wasn't going to go easily. She had some fight left in her still. She was the only hope these children had left.

Her hands had been tied together with a leather strip that looked as if it might have been cut from old horse tackle.

On the downside, the strip was strong, too tough to be ripped. On the upside, leather was a natural material and flexible, so it did give a little if she pulled hard enough. If she could stretch the loop out even half an inch, she might be able to slip her hands through.

She watched Dylan while she worked on that, praying that she succeeded before he found the right spot to get rid of her.

A grim expression sat on his face, his fingers gripping the wheel hard. He kept his attention on the rocky road. Then he suddenly looked at the rearview mirror and swore up a blue streak.

"What is it?"

He stepped on the gas.

She checked the side mirror. Two small dots of light shone in the distance, another car somewhere pretty far behind them.

A slim chance, but it gave her hope, anyway.

She worked on the leather and watched as the car gained on them. She knew who it was, knew it in her heart—Ryder. Even if that made no sense. He knew to come to the old cabin, but he would have no way of knowing where Dylan took her from there. Maybe he was following Dylan's tracks.

She yanked hard on the leather. She had to stay alive long enough for him to reach them.

"Who the hell is that?"

"Probably Border Patrol. I did tell people where I was going," she lied, hoping he would give up.

Dylan swore again then yanked the steering wheel aside and drove off the road. He headed straight south. And they were only maybe five miles from the border.

She yanked at the leather harder, not caring now if he noticed. He was heading into Mexico where Ryder couldn't follow them. He had no jurisdiction there. He was part of some secret commando group. Third-generation military, he'd told her once. And an armed American soldier crossing over into another sovereign nation would be a huge problem.

Something like that could be considered an act of war if some local Mexican politician decided to make a big deal of it to improve his ratings. There was too much friction between the two countries these days over illegal immigration. An incident like this could set off a chain reaction that could damage international relations for years.

Dear God, please let Ryder catch up with us before we cross the border. Dylan must have a boat hidden, or some other way planned to get across the Rio Grande. He wasn't driving like a madman in that direction by accident.

She kept her eyes on the mirror while she whispered encouragement to the children in mixed Spanish and

English. Rosita didn't like the bumpy road and was crying again.

The river glistened darkly ahead of them in the moonlight. They were rapidly nearing the border, and Ryder was still too far behind. No way could he close that distance in time.

She cast a frenetic glance at Dylan. A triumphant smile spread on his face, even as her heart sank.

Chapter Twelve

Ryder could see the border on his GPS unit. No matter how hard he pushed on the gas, he couldn't catch up with the pickup in front of him.

His team was on their way, but this fight he would have to fight alone and now. He had no doubt what Grace's captor intended to do with her. The bodies he'd found in the log cabin told him that the bastard wasn't squeamish. The man had passed the point of no return and he knew it. He wouldn't hesitate at anything at this stage.

The pickup was just a half mile in front of him and slowing suddenly. It stopped. And then disappeared.

Ryder squinted hard, driving full speed ahead. He didn't step on the brake until he reached the area where the pickup had vanished. He drove around in a circle, using his headlights as well as the floodlight attached to his SUV. He noticed a shallow dent in the ground. Just didn't look right, prickling his instincts.

He got out and pulled his gun as he walked over. A perfectly camouflaged trapdoor, he realized after a moment, a rough circle about a dozen feet in diameter. He'd never seen anything like this before, but he wasn't about to waste time on admiring it. He searched for an opening mechanism.

As fast as the pickup had gone through, the driver must have had a remote. But there had to be another way to open the damn thing. He found a metal box buried in the dirt right next to it, connected to the door by cables. Padlocked with a keypad lock. He didn't have time to mess with it, so he shot the padlock off. The controls inside were more sophisticated than he'd expected, but familiar.

Not a trapdoor, after all, but a fancy vehicle lift.

He pulled his SUV right onto the platform, left the door open, pushed the lower button in the box, then jumped back into his car just as it began to rapidly slip underground. Pretty much the most impressive setup he'd seen for a border tunnel.

He kept his weapon out as he waited to reach bottom, which he did rapidly. An endless tunnel stretched in front of him, absolutely professional, a miniature version of a highway tunnel you'd see on any U.S. road. Major money had gone into making this. Then again, the illegal drug and weapons trade was a flourishing business that produced around four hundred billion dollars a year, worldwide. There were countries with worse GDPs, or Gross Domestic Product.

He stepped on the gas and the car shot forward in the tunnel that had a downward angle. The GPS signal disappeared, but he knew roughly when he crossed the border. He was under the river now. And hoped the people who'd dug the tunnel really knew what they were doing.

When the bottom of the tunnel began to curve up, he knew he was nearing the end. He stopped before the elevator shaft and called the platform down using an instrument panel on the wall. Then up he went.

Hurry. Grace could be gone by now. Precious minutes had gone wasted while he'd searched for the entrance to the tunnel.

But when he reached the top, he could see the pickup's disappearing taillights in the distance. He stepped hard on the gas pedal. Grace was in that pickup, and she was in trouble.

When he managed to close the distance sufficiently at last, he stuck his gun out the window and aimed for the back tires. He could only shoot left-handed, since he was behind the wheel.

As bumpy as the ground was, only his third shot hit its aim. The second tire was more accommodating, blowing on the very next shot, and the truck fishtailed before it slowed, then came to a halt eventually, in another couple of yards.

He had no authorization whatsoever to enter the sovereign territory of Mexico. A court martial hung as a very real possibility in his near future.

He couldn't have cared less.

The passenger-side door of the pickup opened. Grace got out, helping two small children to the ground as best she could with her hands tied in front of her. Then the barrel of a gun appeared behind them, followed by someone familiar, someone unexpected. *Dylan.*

Fury burned through Ryder. He'd run the man through the system, dammit. He'd come up squeaky clean.

The man held his weapon to Grace's head. "Throw your gun out the window," he shouted to Ryder.

Ryder did so immediately, but managed to keep the

toss short, so the weapon didn't end up too far from his SUV. Then he carefully reached down to his boot where he'd gotten into the habit of keeping a backup gun. He shoved that into the back of his waistband, counting on Dylan not being able to see him since the SUV's lights were still on.

"Turn off the car, then get out with your hands in the air," Dylan instructed.

Ryder turned the key, but left it in the ignition. He pushed the door open slowly, didn't want to spook the man. "You can take my car. It has a full tank of gas. Just leave Grace and the kids." He lifted his hands, but not too high. "You can just keep driving south."

But Dylan had no intention of doing that. He aimed and squeezed the trigger.

Grace, in some superhero move, vaulted over the kids and knocked into him, causing the bullet to go stray by an inch maybe. But that measly inch made a world of difference in this case.

Dylan knocked her to the ground then immediately aimed at Ryder again, but by then Ryder was ready for him. He pulled his smaller sidearm from behind his back and aimed in the same smooth move.

One shot.

Straight through the head.

Then he ran forward, keeping his weapon ready, even though he knew he wasn't going to need it.

By the time he reached them, Grace had her arms around the crying kids. She had somehow freed herself.

His heart raced like a speeding bullet. He didn't seem to be able to catch his breath. The sight of her was the most wonderful thing he'd ever seen in his life. Then he noticed the blood on her face. "Anybody hurt?"

She shook her head.

He wanted to grab hold of her and then keep holding her for a week or so. But the sooner they got back to the U.S. side of the border, the better. He didn't want to run into any Mexican border guards and have to explain himself.

Especially since—if they'd heard the gunfire—they might just shoot first and ask questions later.

"Come on." He picked up Miguel. "Let's get out of here."

She picked up Rosita and followed him to his SUV. Then he drove out of Mexico as fast as he'd come in, right through the superfancy tunnel.

His phone rang just as he came out on the U.S. side.

"We're at the log cabin," Mo told him. "Nice mess. Where the hell are you?"

"Stay where you are. I'm coming back there. I have Grace and the children." He glanced at his GPS that was working once again. "Found another tunnel. You won't believe this one." And he gave the coordinates.

"We'll check it out in the morning. We're going to have enough on our hands for tonight, cleaning up this mess."

Ryder hung up, then reassured the children that they were going to be fine, all the bad things were over now and they were going to soon see their mother. Only when he succeeded in calming them down did he ask Grace what happened.

She gave him the highlights.

"I can't believe Dylan could be involved in something like this," she said when she finished, shoulders slumped, looking pretty beat.

"You're safe," he said, pretty much the only thing he could think.

"Thank you for coming after us."

The hounds of hell couldn't have held him back.

"Are you going to get into trouble for crossing the border?"

"I don't care."

"Since when? You don't break rules."

Since she'd come to mean more to him than any other woman he'd ever met. But now was not the time to tell her that. Instead, he asked more about how she'd found the children and how Dylan had come into the picture. He could tell that she still had trouble dealing with that.

"If it's any consolation, I didn't see that coming, either," he said as they reached the old log cabin. Several SUVs surrounded it, belonging to his team who were coming through the front door with grim looks on their faces.

"Stay in the car with the kids," he told Grace before he got out to speak to the others.

The inside of the log cabin had scared the soul out of him when he'd first burst in. He'd spent a long, frenetic minute searching for Grace's body in the bloody mess. Grace had seen it already, but she shouldn't have to see it again. And it was definitely too gruesome for the kids.

Mo reached him first. "How are they?"

"Fine." He stepped aside so his friend could see into the SUV, where Grace was cuddling the children who were half-asleep. "No injuries."

Mo's shoulders relaxed. "What are we going to do with those four bodies in there?"

"Let local law enforcement deal with it," Ryder said.

"Did they get anything out of the wire mill boss yet?"

"He lawyered up and clammed up. But I bet he'll talk when he realizes what kind of charges he faces. He'll be begging for a plea bargain."

Mo nodded and dialed. Their mission was a bust at this stage. Too much action had been going on on the Cordero ranch these past few days. Whoever was running the show had probably already switched to plan B, another location.

Border Patrol and the local law could take care of the cleanup and investigation here. Ryder and his team had a more important job. They had to figure out the new location their enemies would choose now and set up surveillance all over again. In time to prevent the terrorists from entering the United States.

He wasn't worried. If there was a team to accomplish that, his team was it.

"Cops are on their way," Mo said, coming after him, stashing his phone away.

"Want to tell us what happened?" Jamie asked.

Ryder gave them a quick update.

"All that rush, and everyone's dead when we get here. Prince Charming off on the rescue all by his tough self." Keith kicked at the dirt. "I feel cheated." He was the youngest man on the team and lived for the excitement of action, hadn't yet seen enough blood to be as wary of it as the others were.

"Not to worry." Ryder clapped him on the shoulder. "There'll be a next time and soon, I'd bet. You just make sure you're ready."

He puffed his chest out. "I was born ready."

Shep shoved him. "You were born an idiot." And the two went at each other in a friendly scuffle.

"The most highly trained soldiers the country has to offer," Jamie said with disgust.

Ryder shook his head.

"I'll take the kids to be checked out at the hospital in Hullett and make sure their mother is notified. I'll have social services meet us there," Mo said. "I'm guessing you'll be bringing Grace?"

"I would, but I doubt she'll let me."

"Guess we know who's wearing the pants in that relationship," Keith said, having broken from Shep.

"There's no relationship."

"You just broke every rule in the book for her." Jamie cast him a skeptical glance. "Do we look stupid?"

Ryder grinned. "Now that you mention it…" And braced for the hit. They were all still riding an adrenaline high, buzzing with energy.

Mo pushed between them. Built like a tank, he wasn't the easiest person to get around.

So Ryder stepped back. "All right, let's get moving. You take the kids." Mo was great with kids. His size and rumbling voice never scared them. They usually treated him like a big teddy bear.

They walked over to get the twins. Of course, Grace immediately said, "I want to go with them. They're scared."

But Ryder found that he was reluctant to let her go just yet. "You need rest. Let me take you home. I have a few more questions, anyway."

And seeing that the kids were, in fact, fine with Mo—Rosita had fallen asleep as he carried her over to his car—she agreed. "My truck."

"Fine. But I'm driving."

She rolled her eyes.

"You've had a rough couple of days," he told her. "I want you to relax."

And she didn't argue further, miracle of miracles.

He glanced around. "And where is your truck, exactly?"

"A little bit down the road in the bushes."

He stared at her. He couldn't believe she'd walked with that brace.

As Mo drove away toward Hullett, Ryder went back to talk to the others for a few minutes, discussed how they would handle the police.

Grace came up behind him. "Thanks for coming."

"You did a good job," Keith said with more admiration in his voice than Ryder would have liked.

"We're leaving," he said, and turned around, swung Grace into his arms and walked down the road in the darkness, ignoring when she protested.

He also ignored the laughter and the mocking whistle calls behind him.

"Put me down!"

"Too late for that."

"Oh, great. You're too worried that your friends might think you're not strong enough to carry me."

"Nah, just don't want to embarrass you. I put you down now, and they'll all think you're too heavy to be carried." He staggered a little to underline his words.

She growled at him. He supposed she'd meant it to be a sound of warning and anger, but he found it irresistibly sexy.

Her truck wasn't that far. He got there too fast, long before he was ready to part with her. She practically leaped from his arms, got in and slammed the door behind her.

"Go that way." She pointed in the opposite direction from the one Mo had taken. "It's a shortcut to the ranch."

He followed the suggestion and drove through the night. She stayed quiet. Probably not feeling too well. She'd been through the blender these past couple of days. The sooner he got her home the better. "Are you sure you're all right? Maybe it wouldn't hurt if a doctor checked you out."

"Nothing he could do for bruises."

"How are you doing with Dylan's death?" He'd never been a great fan of the guy, but the man had been Grace's friend. The betrayal had to hurt.

"Hasn't hit me yet."

He would just have to make sure to be there for her when it did.

He drove on in silence for a while before he said, "Please don't do that ever again. Don't put yourself in danger like that."

She stiffened. "Because I'm not as strong as you are? I'm not all washed-up, you know. I still have something to offer. I can handle it."

"I know you can. But I can't, Grace." He glanced over at her. "A couple of times today, I wasn't sure if I was going to get to you in time."

They had driven several miles, the log cabin no longer visible in the distance. They were out in the middle of nowhere under the endless Texas sky. And it hit him suddenly just how much she meant to him, how easily he could have lost her. He slowed the truck, then stopped it altogether and shut off the engine.

"What's wrong?" She was instantly alert, peering into the darkness.

"Come over here." His voice sounded hoarse. He didn't care. He met her in the middle, where the steering wheel wouldn't impede dragging her onto his lap.

She didn't protest when he folded his arms around her, or when he tasted her lips.

Or when that tentative tasting turned into craving he couldn't slake as he fully claimed her. The adrenaline rush of the chase still hummed through his blood, along with the relief of finding her alive. Sharp need sliced through him, filled him, brought his senses alive.

Need. Heat. Want.

She felt exactly right and perfect in his arms. He claimed her mouth, then kissed his way down her neck as she let her head fall back. She had to have the softest skin in the world. He could spend the rest of his life running his lips over all that velvet.

He adjusted her so she straddled him, her breasts just a short dip of his head away. He tried to be careful with the buttons on her shirt, but a couple went flying, anyway.

When he tugged down her bra and pulled a swollen nipple into his mouth, she moaned his name.

WHATEVER PAIN HER BRUISES caused, pleasure overrode it. An hour ago, she wasn't sure she was going to live through the day. Now she felt more alive than she could ever remember feeling.

She tugged his shirt over his head and ran her seeking fingers over his chest, the hills and valleys of muscles, as she rubbed against his hardness between her legs. He bit back a groan and sucked harder on her nipple.

Desire swirled through her body, hot need. His hands

slipped to her waist, tugging the flimsy material of her shorts away from her body. A hand on each hip, his thumbs massaged the sensitive crease that lead to the V of her thighs.

His mouth switched to the other nipple. Her underwear disappeared at the same time. The man was a wizard at multitasking.

She reached between them and undid his belt. He lifted slightly and shrugged his pants and underwear down in the same move. Then they were flesh to flesh, hard to soft.

And he looked up at her, desperation in his eyes suddenly.

A second passed before her mind surfaced from the sensual haze enough to understand his unspoken question. And then more effort to make her lips say the words. "I'm on the pill."

He flashed her a profound look of gratitude. "I'm clean. We get regularly tested for everything."

The secret team he worked on, she thought, but was too distracted to ponder that now. "Same here." Not the testing, but she was clean. The men in her life had been few and far between, and she'd always insisted on tangible protection. Until now.

His hands slid under her, lifted her up, over him. Then he stilled, letting her take control of what would happen next. With his swollen tip at her opening, she didn't hesitate long.

She lowered her body onto his and moaned with pleasure.

They both held their breath for a second, against the onslaught of sensations. Then he began to gently rock under her.

Pressure built quickly, her body more than ready.

One of his clever hands moved up to her breast, the other between her legs, his thumb finding the very spot that ached for his touch.

They rocked together, moving closer and closer to the edge of the precipice. Her fingers tangled in the short hair at his nape. When he sent her over, she cried out his name, and through her own pleasure felt him let go at last and pulsate deep inside her.

Their harsh breathing filled the cab as she fell against him, utterly spent.

Pure bliss surrounded her, the likes of which she hadn't felt in a long time, if ever. But the sense of "right" didn't last long. Because all of a sudden she remembered.

And yanked her body back hard, making him wince. "You're getting married!" She tried to scramble off him, but he held her in place.

"It's not like that. What I meant was that I want to marry, in general."

She stared at him. "What do you mean in general? As in there isn't a specific woman?"

He pressed against her. "Oh, there's a woman. Just not the kind I expected."

She was pretty much speechless at that. "I'm not ever getting married," she said. Not that he'd asked. She cleared her throat, suddenly embarrassed. "Just to be clear."

"Okay," he said with a goofy grin.

"Okay?"

"Whatever you're willing to give, I'm taking."

Ryder McKay was a dangerous man, she thought, not for the first time. She could see herself falling in love with him. Even if she knew that doing something stupid like that would bring her nothing but pain eventually.

Her judgment was appallingly bad when it came to men. As demonstrated by Dylan.

"I'm not going to hurt you. Ever," he promised, then kissed the tip of one nipple, then the other.

Electricity zinged through her. "Stop that," she protested weakly. Then she drew a long breath. "This was—" she swallowed "—the result of an adrenaline rush. A celebration of survival."

"Whatever you need to tell yourself." He grinned at her.

"Just don't expect it to happen again." She tried to move away but, again, he wouldn't let her.

"I didn't think you were the type to run from reality."

"Reality is, we don't belong together."

"How about we give it a try, anyway?"

"You are very stubborn."

"You're no slouch yourself." He grinned.

"It'll never work."

"Why?"

"For one, I'm going back home soon."

"There's no need for a good veterinarian in Hullett?" he challenged.

"You'll go away when whatever it is you're doing here is done," she countered.

"I might go away for missions from time to time, but with all the trouble along the border, our placement here is permanent."

"I'm…" She pressed her lips together, unsure how to explain. "Damaged." She drew another deep breath. "You're a warrior, and I'm broken in so many ways. I'm not a warrior's mate."

"You're perfect." His tone was sure and fierce.

Embarrassed by the frank admiration in his gaze, she shifted. And felt him stiffen inside her. He pressed against her, and just like that a tingle of pleasure started where their bodies were joined. "We weren't going to do this again," she said, her voice not nearly as sure as she would have liked.

"You said that. I'm here to point out the error of your thinking." He bent his head to her nipple again, his hands squeezing her buttocks as he gathered her closer.

SHE WOKE IN HER BED, with him, and for this second time she actually made it to the bathroom. The first time they'd woken, he made love to her again.

He wasn't far behind her this time, either. And more than ready.

She tore her gaze away.

"I can't help wanting you." He didn't sound the least apologetic.

If she were smart, she would have found some indignation somewhere deep down and sent him away. Instead, she said, "I'm taking a shower."

"Me, too." A suggestive grin split his lips.

"Maybe later. First you're making us breakfast."

"Great idea. And then you'll owe me. Word of warning—I always collect." He padded away with a self-satisfied grin.

She tried not to stare at his well-formed behind as he went, but she failed.

She set the water in the shower a few degrees colder than usual. She'd never known need like this. It bordered on the ridiculous. She needed to focus on something else or they would never leave the ranch again.

She cleaned up and dressed, wondering how Molly was taking the news of Dylan's death. She must have been told by now. Grace wasn't sure if going over there would help or make everything worse, since she was involved in his death. Maybe she would give Molly some time. She couldn't stand the thought that their friendship might be affected. Then she thought of the kids, wished she knew how they were doing. She wanted to ask Ryder to call in and check, but he had the news ready when she walked into the kitchen.

"Border patrol has the children at the crossing station. They already alerted their mother. Esperanza will be there to pick them up around noon. Want to go and see her?"

She looked up into his desert-honey eyes and fell in love. Oh, man. Okay. Wow. Nobody had ever told her it could happen like this. This unexpectedly. This quickly. She sat down hard onto the chair.

"I'd love to go." She looked at the eggs, at anything but him. "Sure."

"Grace?"

"Aren't you going to eat?"

He put his own plate down on the table across from her. "You look a little strange. Are you okay?"

"Umm…mmm." She made some noise of affirmation around the food in her mouth.

"Last night. I wasn't too… You've been recently hurt."

"It was fine." Her cheeks flamed.

"Fine?" He sounded disappointed.

She choked on her eggs. Managed to get them down, then escaped to the sink with her empty plate.

Thankfully, he didn't push. When he was done with

his breakfast, he took a shower. "I should probably go into the office," he said when he came back down. "After last night, there'll be some questions I'll have to answer."

"Sure," she said quickly, with relief. She needed some space to gather her thoughts.

"I'll see you at the border crossing at noon?"

"I'll be there."

He strode up to her and pressed a hot kiss on her lips, flashed her another questioning look, but then he walked away.

Chapter Thirteen

"The Mexican authorities found the body of a Dylan Rogers across the border. He was shot last night, apparently."

"Yes, sir. I'm sorry, sir," Ryder apologized, even if he knew he would do the same all over again. The team leader thing wasn't nearly as important to him as Grace. Nothing was.

"This wouldn't have anything to do with that personal business of yours, would it?" the Colonel asked.

"I'm sorry, sir," he said again.

"You caused a big headache here, soldier. I hope she's worth it."

"Yes, sir."

A few seconds passed on the other end. "Congratulations, soldier."

He must have missed something. "I don't understand, sir."

"I'm making you the team leader of the SDDU's Texas office. Don't disappoint me."

"No, sir."

"You were always an excellent solider, McKay, but something was missing."

"Sir?" He had no idea what the man was talking about.

"You always performed your duty, followed all the rules, crossed your *t*'s and dotted your *i*'s and then some. But last night's business showed me you also have a heart. A heart is important in a leader."

"Yes, sir."

"I want to be invited to the wedding," the man said before he hung up on Ryder.

That was the Colonel for you. You could be a tough commando solider all you want, but the man could still pull the rug from under you without half trying.

The wedding.

It sounded right.

Grace Cordero. Who would have thought? She was the exact opposite of the kind of woman he'd planned on marrying. Back when he'd been clueless and stupid.

"She's the one," Ryder said out loud, without meaning to.

Ray was at the hospital, having his cast checked. The others were out, scouting the land, trying to identify the traffickers' plan B. For something this big, they would have one. Possibly even a plan C. The team's mission was to stay one step ahead of the bad guys.

"Which one?" Mo, the only other guy at the office, asked, lost in his computer. Then he did pause, looked up, his damaged eyebrow sliding way up his forehead. "*The* one?"

Ryder gave a careful nod and braced himself for merciless ribbing.

"So Grace Cordero is your Vicky?" Mo wanted to clarify.

"Grace is my Grace." He was hoping to forget the whole Vicky nonsense.

And instead of Mo throwing it into his face and making fun of him, the man gave a wistful sigh. "Good for you."

Ryder stared at his friend. *That was it?*

"You two are right together. I see how you look at each other. It's nice."

Okay, where did that come from? Mo didn't have a romantic bone in his body. He wasn't a ladies' man, tended to get tongue-tied. But he was great with kids, gentle as anything. Maybe because of his own rough beginnings.

Moses Mann. Named Moses by his adoptive parents because he'd been rescued from the river as a baby. His birth parents had put him in a bag and dropped him from a bridge.

The man shrugged. "You get older, you start thinking about things."

Huh. They stared at each other for a second, then looked away at the same time. Neither was the type to do the whole, sharing feelings thing.

Ryder pushed to his feet. "I have to go to the crossing station. I have a date with Child Protective Services and Grace."

The ride over was too short to think everything over. He wanted Grace, for more than a casual affair. But how would he convince her to agree? She wanted away from here. She wanted a new life in the city of Bryan. He was pretty sure she was dealing with some PTSD. She wouldn't want any sort of action/adventure to be part of her life, and his life consisted of nothing but.

And yet they were going to find a compromise, because he wasn't going to let go of her.

She was already there when he arrived, in the interview room where they all waited for him. She'd brought a goodie bag for each child: a pretty dress, sweets and a teddy bear for Rosita; sneakers, sweets and a toy car for Miguel. The kids were looking at her as if she were Mrs. Santa Claus.

Everyone was smiling, including the social worker.

"Mr. McKay. Heard a lot about you. Thank you for what you did to save these children." She held out her hand.

He shook it. "Mostly Grace's doing." She was the one who wouldn't let go, even when she had to put her life on the line.

"From what I understand, the mother has arrived. Ready to walk over?"

The kids hung on to Grace, an odd thing, really, since she was the only one who couldn't speak their language. But children were perceptive, and they figured out that she cared for them deeply. They somehow knew that she was the one who'd saved them.

As they walked outside, Rosita reached for Ryder's hand, too, linking him and Grace together. And their eyes met over the little girl. Grace looked away first.

Okay, this was not the time, but they would definitely have to talk later.

A Border Patrol officer joined them to escort them around the long line at the window. They cleared Mexican customs in a few minutes. Calls had been made already, everything set up for this.

The children spotted Esperanza first and screamed with joy as they rushed to their mother. The woman bent and caught them, buried her face against her twins, sobbing loudly, asking them if they were all right. She wore all black. The call that had given her the time and place for today's meeting had also informed her of her husband's passing.

An older woman stood behind her, the family resemblance obvious.

"Have you heard anything about the girls who were rescued from the mill?" Grace asked.

"They'll be returned home by the end of the week. No charges. They were brought here against their will, snagged off the streets in their villages. Smuggled across the border in vans. Apparently there were more, but two suffocated on the way." He would have loved to have ten minutes privately with the bastards who ran that business, but they were already in police custody.

"Then Mikey Mitzner will be arrested?" She turned to him.

"Already in the can," he told her with satisfaction. "The man you beat up in the basement gave him up. Mitzner allowed the use of the mill to house smuggled people in transit, for a share of the profits."

The children turned to their grandmother for another flurry of hugs and, after long minutes, Esperanza walked forward to Grace, looking back after nearly every step to make sure the children were still there.

"Muchas gracias, señora." She took Grace's hand and held it.

"De nada." What Grace couldn't say in Spanish, she put into her smile.

"Gracias, señor."

Ryder assured her that no thanks were necessary and expressed his and Grace's condolences. The young woman nodded, tears in her eyes, but a smile on her lips. The children and their grandmother came up behind her.

The wrinkled old woman looked at him, then at Grace, then said a few words before she turned to walk away with her family.

"What did she say?" Grace wanted to know.

"She's the medicine woman in her village." He looked after her, stunned. "She said we'll have a long and happy life and lots of children together."

Since Grace didn't want that, he expected her to protest and scrambled to marshal a few good points in favor of all that. But instead of protesting, a smile stretched her face.

"You don't hate the idea?" he asked with caution.

She tilted her head, searching his face. "Do you?"

He didn't have to think about it. "Best idea I've heard all…ever."

He stepped forward. She stepped toward him and they met in the middle, sharing a hot kiss. People coming across the border cheered, approving whistles splitting the air.

"I think we're making a spectacle of ourselves," she murmured against his lips.

"I don't mind." He stole another kiss.

But she pulled away. "Aren't you here in an official capacity?"

He shook his head. "Now you're a stickler for rules?"

They walked back across the border together. The social worker was already gone.

He walked her to her pickup at the far end of the lot, happiness soaring through him. He pulled her to him and kissed her with all the love and passion he felt for her. The kiss left both of them breathless.

"Ryder," she protested weakly.

He flashed her a grin. "My shift just ended." He nudged her toward the pickup. "Get in."

Her eyes went round, her cheeks turning pink. "Not in a crowded parking lot!"

He laughed out loud. "I'm going home with you."

"What about your SUV?"

"I'll ask Mo to pick it up. I need some one on one time with you right now."

She blushed even harder. Then got in. "Okay. But I'm driving."

Bigger battles lay ahead, so he went around to the passenger seat. "The kids are negotiable," he said, hoping she got the hint that the two of them together wasn't. No way was he going to let her walk away from him.

"To be honest," she said casually as she started the engine. "I think I'd be okay with kids."

Pleasure flooded him. "Bryan is not that far. We can make this work."

She glanced at him. "I'll go back to Bryan when I need to for exams but—" she shook her head "—I can't leave the ranch now. I have patients here. I have a bushel of cats."

"I got a promotion. I'm going to be the team leader. Permanently stationed here."

"Are you ever going to be able to tell me what it is exactly that you're doing?"

"Probably not." He thought for a second. "Can you handle that?"

"I'm not a great fan of mysterious government men with secret agendas. So, just tell me what you can."

"I've done a lot of things, working mostly overseas until recently—gathering information, then acting on it."

"Like a spy?"

"More like a cross between a spy and a commando soldier."

She considered his words, taking her time.

The long silence made him nervous. "Do you think you could come to accept that someday?" Because he definitely had long-term plans for her in his life.

A slow smile spread across her face. "I could fall in love with you, Ryder McKay."

Could? "What would it take to push you over the edge?"

She wiggled her eyebrows in a suggestive manner that sent his blood racing.

"Take the back roads that go through your land," he ordered.

"The county road is faster. We're almost at the ranch, anyway."

He unclicked his seat belt and slid over, dropped his lips right to her ear and nibbled the sensitive lobe before he said, "I don't think we're going to make it."

SHE WOKE TO A GLORIOUS morning, happier than she could remember ever being. Ryder was in the shower. She padded downstairs to start coffee. She was grabbing her mug from the dishwasher when the phone rang. Shane.

"Sorry for calling so early, Gracie honey. I'm glad you're okay. I want to swing by this morning to talk about some of that stuff that went down last night. Mostly about Dylan. Wanted to make sure you were home before I headed out that way."

She hesitated for a moment, looking through the window at the endless ranch. "I'm going to lay Tommy to rest this morning." The time seemed right somehow, suddenly.

"Of course," Shane said. "We can talk whenever you're ready."

Ryder was coming into the kitchen by the time she hung up. He wore blue jeans with a black shirt and Tommy's boots. He wore the spurs, too, jingling all the way down. He flashed her a sheepish look. "There's just something satisfying about spurs. In a John Wayne kind of way. I'll take them off in a minute."

"If you don't watch it, you're going to turn into a Texan one of these days."

He gave a slow nod, watching her. "It's the kind of place that gets right under your skin, isn't it?"

She watched him do his manly cowboy swagger as he came to her, and her heart turned over in her chest.

"I'm going to lay Tommy to rest today," she told him, feeling at peace with the decision.

He gave her a gentle kiss and gathered her into his arms.

"You probably have to get to work," she mumbled into his shirt.

She'd always meant to say goodbye to Tommy privately. But suddenly she didn't want to be alone.

"I'd like to stay if you don't mind." Ryder kissed her forehead and kept holding her.

She laid her cheek against his shoulder. "Okay."

"Would you mind if the guys came out, too? They've all been in the military one time or the other. They've gotten to know you and they like you. I'm pretty sure they'd want to be here, unless you'd rather not have anyone."

"The guys are fine," she said, and meant it. They were the type of men Tommy would have been friends with. They were like brothers to Ryder and Ryder was like… Ryder was the man she was in love with. "Okay."

He sat her down and made some calls, then fixed her breakfast. After they cleaned up the dishes together, she changed into the best outfit she'd brought with her, black jeans, black cowboy boots, then put on Tommy's favorite shirt at the last second instead of her own.

"Let me get these spurs off." He bent to take care of them.

"You're good as you are," she told him. "I think Tommy would like it."

She lifted the urn from the mantel and cradled it with her right arm. Ryder took her other hand and they headed out, crossing the back pasture together to the far meadow.

Mo, Jamie and the others showed up just as she started reciting the twenty-third psalm, Gramps's favorite prayer. From the corner of her eye, she saw the sheriff's car pull up her drive. Shane and Mattie got out. Then Kenny, the Pebble Creek sheriff, came. Then more trucks with Tommy's friends. Even old man Murray and Henry showed up.

Molly didn't come. Grace shut her eyes for a second. She didn't want to lose that friendship. She would have to deal with that. But not now.

People came across the field, following each other in a line, gathering around her. Mattie started singing "Amazing Grace." Others joined in.

Grace stood facing the sun, golden glow gilding the ranch in otherworldly beauty, her arms wrapped tightly around the urn.

"You were the best brother anyone could wish," she said when the song ended. "You were a good friend, a good soldier, an amazing person who should still be here. I'm never going to forget you, Tommy, I swear." She swallowed hard. "I'm going to try to be like you were, so you can be proud of me. Because I'm so damn proud of you." She lifted off the top as a gust of wind rushed across the land. "I love you, Tommy."

And then with a soft sweep of her arm, she let him fly on the wind, over the land they both loved.

She stumbled back, fairly blinded by tears. Ryder's strong arms folded around her. Then she felt another hand on her shoulder, a soft squeeze. Others moved in for hugs and comforting words.

And little by little her empty heart seemed to refill.

She blinked back her tears as she looked at the gathered men and women. This was where she belonged. With these people, on this land, with this man.

He stood by her side, holding her hand, leaning to her ear to whisper, "I love you, Grace."

She turned into his embrace, and didn't care who was watching. "I love you, too, city slicker."

Epilogue

The two men at the back of the funeral crowd stood apart from the others, talking under their breath.

"This will be the end of it?" It better be, too much money was on the line. Too much money and his reputation. His life really, considering the type of people he was dealing with this time. Coyote looked at his local connection, hoping to hell the man was up to the task.

"They got Dylan. They found two tunnels. They have Mikey Mitzner in jail. They'll think they broke the back of the operation." Kenny, the not-altogether-upstanding sheriff of Pebble Creek, scanned the mourners. "Although, I don't like the look of Gracie with that government snoop. Looks like he might be sticking around."

"We'll avoid the Cordero ranch for a while, until things die down."

Kenny nodded.

Coyote scanned the small group of outsiders who supposedly worked on some project or other for Border Protection. Tough-looking bunch, that one. Worth keeping an eye on. If there was more trouble, it'd be coming from that quarter. He would just have to make sure that didn't happen.

"Rogers had to be sacrificed?" Not that he minded.

The man hadn't been nearly as conscienceless as he liked to work with. Dylan Rogers had been new to the game and sometimes hesitant. His football hero past pulled him back. He liked the money, but had never fully embraced the criminal lifestyle.

"He was the weakest link. Once I handed that Chevy emblem over to Gracie and the man snooping after Paco, Dylan's days were numbered." Kenny puffed out his chest, looking very proud of himself.

He'd owed Dylan Rogers money. More than a little. The man's death had a neat way of wiping out that debt. Coyote watched the sheriff, but didn't say anything about that.

"Going into human trafficking was stupid of him. Shouldn't have done that," the man said, as if trying to justify the betrayal. "We make plenty of money on drug running. He didn't have to be so greedy." He swore under his breath. "And hooking up with freaking Mikey. Who's gonna run the mill if they put Mikey away? A lot of people are gonna go jobless around here. The idiots never thought of that."

Coyote nodded. The local economy didn't really interest him. He found the sheriff's small-town notions and alliances quaint.

The sheriff didn't know it yet, but he'd be involved in human trafficking and worse before this game was over. Some big players were coming in; big money was on the line. Failure wasn't an option.

"Rogers has a sister. You think he told her anything about where his extra money was coming from? They own that ranch together." Loose ends had to be tied up, and quickly.

"No way. Molly would have been over at CBP the

day she found out about it. A born Girl Scout that one. But pretty. Lonely now, too. I'll make sure to look in on her."

"She here?"

Kenny shook his head. "Heard she was messed up over Dylan's death." A speculative look came over the man's face. He was probably wondering how soon he could go over to offer the woman a shoulder to cry on.

Coyote shrugged. Where the sheriff went for romance was none of his concern. As long as it didn't interfere with their business.

"We need to cut back on shipping for a while. Ease it to a trickle. Make the authorities think that they scared us off," he said.

The creepy smile slid off the sheriff's face. "That'll cut into the money some."

He was always short on funds. Big fan of online gambling and cockfights for which he regularly traveled to the other side of the border.

No conscience whatsoever and money problems. Unlike Dylan, the sheriff was fairly easy to manage, Coyote thought. He could have used a half dozen more associates just like the man.

"You'll make the money back later. I'm setting up something big."

"How big?"

"Biggest deal we've done yet."

The sheriff brightened at that prospect. "Some new drug?"

"Don't worry about that part. What we ship is my responsibility. You make sure it gets through all smooth and safe."

"So we cut back for now so CBP goes away?"

"Exactly."

"I'll keep an eye on Rogers's sister in the meanwhile."

"You do that. And if it looks like she knows more than what she's let on so far…"

"I'll take care of it."

Yes, he would, and without any hesitation. He would take care of the problem, then cover it up, make it disappear. The sheriff had never been the least squeamish that way.

* * * * *

COMING NEXT MONTH from Harlequin® Intrigue®
AVAILABLE AUGUST 7, 2012

#1365 GAGE
The Lawmen of Silver Creek Ranch
Delores Fossen
After faking his death to protect his family, CIA agent Gage Ryland is forced to secretly return from the grave to save his ex, Lynette Herrington, who's carrying a secret of her own.

#1366 SECRET ASSIGNMENT
Cooper Security
Paula Graves
On a visit to a private island, an archivist stumbles onto an invasion, forcing her to work with the handsome caretaker to learn who will stop at nothing to gain access to the island—and why.

#1367 KANSAS CITY COWBOY
The Precinct: Task Force
Julie Miller
Sheriff Boone Harrison and police psychologist Kate Kilpatrick couldn't be more different. But trusting each other is the only way to catch a killer...and find a second chance at love.

#1368 MOMMY MIDWIFE
Cassie Miles
Nine months after a night she'll never forget, a pregnant midwife must trust the baby's father, a man she barely knows, to rescue her from the madman who wants her baby.

#1369 COPY THAT
HelenKay Dimon
A girl-next-door gets sucked into a dangerous new life when a wounded border patrol agent lands on her doorstep, with gunmen hot on his trail.

#1370 HER COWBOY AVENGER
Thriller
Kerry Connor
Her husband's murder turned her into an outcast and a suspect—and the only man who can help her is the tall, dark cowboy she thought she'd never see again.

You can find more information on upcoming Harlequin® titles, free excerpts and more at www.Harlequin.com.

HICNM0712

REQUEST YOUR FREE BOOKS!
2 FREE NOVELS PLUS 2 FREE GIFTS!

❧ Harlequin®

INTRIGUE®

BREATHTAKING ROMANTIC SUSPENSE

YES! Please send me 2 FREE Harlequin Intrigue® novels and my 2 FREE gifts (gifts are worth about $10). After receiving them, if I don't wish to receive any more books, I can return the shipping statement marked "cancel." If I don't cancel, I will receive 6 brand-new novels every month and be billed just $4.49 per book in the U.S. or $5.24 per book in Canada. That's a saving of at least 14% off the cover price! It's quite a bargain! Shipping and handling is just 50¢ per book in the U.S. and 75¢ per book in Canada.* I understand that accepting the 2 free books and gifts places me under no obligation to buy anything. I can always return a shipment and cancel at any time. Even if I never buy another book, the two free books and gifts are mine to keep forever.

182/382 HDN FEQ2

Name _____ (PLEASE PRINT)

Address _____ Apt. #

City _____ State/Prov. _____ Zip/Postal Code

Signature (if under 18, a parent or guardian must sign)

Mail to the **Reader Service:**
IN U.S.A.: P.O. Box 1867, Buffalo, NY 14240-1867
IN CANADA: P.O. Box 609, Fort Erie, Ontario L2A 5X3

Not valid for current subscribers to Harlequin Intrigue books.

**Are you a subscriber to Harlequin Intrigue books
and want to receive the larger-print edition?
Call 1-800-873-8635 or visit www.ReaderService.com.**

* Terms and prices subject to change without notice. Prices do not include applicable taxes. Sales tax applicable in N.Y. Canadian residents will be charged applicable taxes. Offer not valid in Quebec. This offer is limited to one order per household. All orders subject to credit approval. Credit or debit balances in a customer's account(s) may be offset by any other outstanding balance owed by or to the customer. Please allow 4 to 6 weeks for delivery. Offer available while quantities last.

Your Privacy—The Reader Service is committed to protecting your privacy. Our Privacy Policy is available online at www.ReaderService.com or upon request from the Reader Service.

We make a portion of our mailing list available to reputable third parties that offer products we believe may interest you. If you prefer that we not exchange your name with third parties, or if you wish to clarify or modify your communication preferences, please visit us at www.ReaderService.com/consumerschoice or write to us at Reader Service Preference Service, P.O. Box 9062, Buffalo, NY 14269. Include your complete name and address.

Harlequin®

ROMANTIC
SUSPENSE

CINDY DEES

takes you on a wild journey to find the truth
in her new miniseries

Code X

Aiden McKay is more than just an ordinary man. As part of
an elite secret organization, Aiden was genetically enhanced
to increase his lung capacity and spend extended time under
water. He is a committed soldier, focused and dedicated
to his job. But when Aiden saves impulsive free spirit
Sunny Jordan from drowning she promptly overturns his
entire orderly, solitary world.

As the danger creeps closer, Adien soon realizes Sunny is the
target...but can he save her in time?

Breathless Encounter

Find out this August!

plus
**BONUS
STORY
INSIDE!**

Look out for a reader-favorite bonus story included in each
Harlequin Romantic Suspense book this August!

www.Harlequin.com

HRS27786

Werewolf and elite U.S. Navy SEAL, Matt Parker, must set aside his prejudices and partner with beautiful Fae Sienna McClare to find a magic orb that threatens to expose the secret nature of his entire team.

Harlequin® Nocturne presents the debut of beloved author Bonnie Vanak's new miniseries, PHOENIX FORCE.

Enjoy a sneak preview of THE COVERT WOLF, available August 2012 from Harlequin® Nocturne.

Sienna McClare was Fae, accustomed to open air and fields. Not this boxy subway car.

As the oily smell of fear clogged her nostrils, she inhaled deeply, tried thinking of tall pines waving in the wind, the chatter of birds and a deer cropping grass. A wolf watching a deer, waiting. Prey. Images of fangs flashing, tearing, wet sounds…

No!

She fought the panic freezing her blood. And was gradually able to push the fear down into a dark spot deep inside her. The stench of Draicon werewolf clung to her like cheap perfume.

Sienna hated glamouring herself as a Draicon werewolf, but it was necessary if she was going to find the Orb of Light. Someone had stolen the Orb from her colony, the Los Lobos Fae. A Draicon who'd previously been seen in the area was suspected. Sienna had eagerly seized the chance to help when asked because finding it meant she would no longer be an outcast. The Fae had cast her out when she turned twenty-one because she was the bastard child of a sweet-faced Fae and a Draicon killer. But if she found the Orb, Sienna could return to the only home she'd known. It also meant she could recover her lost memories.

Every time she tried searching for her past, she met with a closed door. Who was she? Which side ruled her?

Fae or Draicon?

Draicon, no way in hell.

Sensing someone staring, she glanced up, saw a man across the aisle. He was heavily muscled and radiated power and confidence. Yet he also had the face of a gentle warrior. Sienna's breath caught. She felt a stir of sexual chemistry.

He was as lonely and grief stricken as she was. Her heart twisted. Who had hurt this man? She wanted to go to him, comfort him and ease his sorrow. Sienna smiled.

An odd connection flared between them. Sienna locked her gaze to his, desperately needing someone who understood.

Then her nostrils flared as she caught his scent. Hatred boiled to the surface. Not a man. Draicon.

The enemy.

Find out what happens next in THE COVERT WOLF by Bonnie Vanak.

Available August 2012 from Harlequin® Nocturne wherever books are sold.

Copyright © 2012 by Bonnie Vanak

HNEXP0812